PICTURING *the* DARK

LINDA COTTON JEFFRIES

SUNBURY
P R E S S ®
Mechanicsburg, PA USA

Published by Sunbury Press, Inc.
Mechanicsburg, Pennsylvania

SUNBURY
P R E S S ®
www.sunburypress.com

For information about special discounts for bulk purchases, please contact Sunbury Press Orders Dept. at (855) 338-8359 or orders@sunburypress.com.

To request one of our authors for speaking engagements or book signings, please contact Sunbury Press Publicity Dept. at publicity@sunburypress.com.

FIRST SUNBURY PRESS EDITION: March 2023

Set in Adobe Garamond | Interior design by Crystal Devine | Cover by Lawrence Knorr | Edited by Taylor Berger-Knorr.

Publisher's Cataloging-in-Publication Data
Names: Jeffries, Linda Cotton, author.
Title: Picturing the dark / Linda Cotton Jeffries.
Description: First trade paperback edition. | Mechanicsburg, PA : Sunbury Press, 2023.
Summary: After surviving a dangerous attack in the spring, August finds Audrey Markum facing her attacker's trial at the same time her friend's baby has been kidnapped. Desperately searching for clues with her friend Detective Rodriguez, they know that the statistics are against them. Audrey wishes for her assailant's trial to speed ahead while simultaneously hoping to stretch out the time they have to locate the tiny infant. Something tells her though, that she can't have it both ways.
Identifiers: ISBN : 979-8-88819-063-0 (paperback) | ISBN : 979-8-88819-064-7 (ePub).
Subjects: FICTION / Mystery & Detective / Women Sleuths | FICTION / Action & Adventure | FICTION / Crime.

Product of the United States of America
0 1 1 2 3 5 8 13 21 34 55

Continue the Enlightenment!

For David and all our family both near and far.

CHAPTER

1

Julius Dudnyk told himself he could live with the micromanagement. After all, that had been going on for years. The "Did you do this?" and the "What about that?" The badgering made up a constant background hum in the time he spent at home, a white noise machine tuned to the sound of her voice. What he was struggling with now, though, was the crying.

It had abated briefly, during tax season when his wife's working days were filled with numbers and returns that she completed with the same ruthless attention to detail that she brought to her housekeeping. Although never seen in person, clients paid top dollar for the meticulous detail she brought to her work, seeking out every loophole and carefully hiding untoward amounts of money. They prized her work and her discretion equally as word of mouth circled her name throughout the more questionable echelons of Pittsburgh society.

He realized that it was only very slowly, over many years, that his wife's peculiarities had truly come to light. For instance, he had never noticed that every item in their home was dusted, scrubbed, or polished on a calculated rotation, a schedule that he only discovered two years ago when she screamed in alarm after he shifted a table to hook up a new television. It was disturbing, of course, that glimpse into a magnificent mind bound by fears and restrictions and limitations that he had never imagined in the young woman he once courted. But then there were so many things that he hadn't known about her. She had still been living in the world when they met, a bright face in his company's hierarchy. He'd fallen for her immediately and then courted and married her in a whirlwind that his mother never really forgave him for. No one wants to admit that their parents were right, but as his wife Hannah had withdrawn further and further from the world, he knew that his mother's suspicions had been well-founded. For the past five years, Hannah's obsession had focused on children.

Cancer treatment that his wife had received as a child had left her infertile, and although the adoption agencies dripped with understanding and concern when they told their tale, nonetheless, they still sang the same tune. Older children, siblings, and children with disabilities were all available, but he'd found himself resisting those options. He sensed that he and his wife probably didn't have the wherewithal to handle more specialized cases. So, they waited. But for a baby, the weeks of waiting had turned into months, the months into years. And after the latest false alarm, the most recent dashing of her hopes, his wife's sobbing had become unbearable. He watched her now as she moved around the kitchen, methodically picking items up off the counter and wiping underneath them, returning them to their precise locations, before dabbing at her eyes and moving to the next section to repeat the careful action.

He stood up from the breakfast table, pocketed his phone and keys, and made a decision. He loved her too much to let this pain continue. He would get her a damn baby, whatever it took, before both of them found themselves stark raving mad.

Oscar eased his truck up the short driveway until it was nearly touching his mother-in-law's sedan. If he didn't want the nosey neighbor complaining about his hitch hanging over the sidewalk, he had to make it tight. Given that bad knees had prevented Cecelia from driving her car for several months, he'd had plenty of practice with the maneuver. He felt good, he realized, as he turned the key, and the truck grew silent. He was tired, of course, but it had been a good day at work today. As an electrical lineman, his schedule could be crazy, especially with summer storms blowing up all the time. That made days like today, spent installing lines for a new housing development, precious. A straight shift, a good team, what more could a person ask for?

With a contented sigh, he gathered the big bucket of chicken in one arm and the bag of sides in the other and moved through the open garage to the kitchen door. It wasn't locked, so that made things even easier. He set the food on the wide, messy counter before stepping quietly into the living room. Not surprisingly, there was his wife Sandy, fast asleep on the sofa, one baby nestled in her arms while the other lay sleeping in the nearby crib. He gently touched the first sleeping child's foot before stepping toward his wife. God, she looked beautiful, he thought. Maybe not in anyone else's eyes at the moment, but to him, she did. Having let loose of the nipple, the baby's mouth gaped open, and he could hear a soft snore. He lifted her carefully out of his wife's arms. Even asleep, Sandy had a death grip on the infant, making it no small feat to separate the two while leaving both of them sleeping. He noticed that this baby's tiny foot had a small freckle on the bottom, so he knew she was Martha. He had thought as much. He felt like he was finally learning to tell the twins apart, but the freckle offered confirmation. He nuzzled her warm neck before laying her down in the crib. Then he saw her open her eyes a slit. Spotting her sister Rose, Martha reached out a tiny hand to clasp her sister's thumb. Then they were both asleep again. It never quit amazing him, the bond that the two had.

After one more look at the babies, Oscar turned to his wife, pulling her blouse closed over the red, sore-looking breast. She opened her eyes to him then, and he lowered his mouth to kiss hers. "How's Mama today?" He asked as he sat down on the sofa next to her. She rearranged her nursing bra and shirt with a tired, casual motion before leaning against him and taking his hand in hers.

"What time is it? Should I be making some dinner for us? I was going to have Mom watch the girls while I went to the grocery store, but her friend came by and persuaded her to go to a movie, so . . ." She turned her wrist to look, but there was no watch sitting on it.

He kissed the inside of her arm and then laid it down gently. "It doesn't matter. I picked up some dinner for us, figured you'd be tired and hungry." He looked again at the crib. "I think they're out. Maybe we could risk sitting down at the table for a change?"

She grinned as he pulled her up, and they both paused to look at the sleeping infants. "Wouldn't that be a wonder? Sounds great," she whispered. There was a second crib up in the nursery, but since the twin girls seemed to sleep best when they were together, they'd settled on the current arrangement. At least for these first few months, it seemed to be working.

In the kitchen, Oscar and Sandy did a familiar dance as one retrieved plates and silverware while the other filled two glasses. Once they'd settled everything on the battered, old, wooden table, Oscar pulled out Sandy's chair and then paused to help her push it in before settling into his seat. When the leg of his chair made an unexpectedly loud scraping sound, they both held their breath and listened. But the quiet continued, and they let their shoulders relax a bit.

"So really, how was today, Sandy? The babies and your mom?" He chose a couple of chicken pieces off the stack and then began dishing out some mashed potatoes as she followed suit.

"They were great. They both fed and napped in the morning and then again this afternoon. I just wish I wasn't quite so sore." She lifted the blouse away from her breast slightly. "Will you help me to remember to put some cream on once we're through eating?"

"Of course." He gave her a silly, smoldering look over the plate of food, and Sandy had no choice but to laugh.

"Keep your shorts on there, pal-of-mine." She handed him the small container of gravy.

"They're on, believe me. It's just nice to see you smile." He reached across the table and squeezed her hand before resuming his meal. "And how was your mom? I'm surprised her friend was able to get her out of the house."

"Well, she sat for most of the day first." Sandy lowered her arms as the frustration washed over her. "I get that it's a tough decision to have the knee replacements done, but when you're in that much pain and hardly moving because of it, I think it's past time."

"I'm with you there."

"Plus, it's so weird for her not to be out back in her studio painting."

"How long has it been, do you think?"

"I'm not sure, at least five or six months? It's just not like her, and I think it adds to the overall crappy way that she's feeling." Sandy's voice softened then. "But she sure does love our girls, Oscar. When Rosey starts that panting/crying routine, Mom can always soothe her back out of it. It's sweet."

"I think your mom's just waiting until things feel more settled with them before she's going to feel comfortable looking after herself."

"You're probably right, but when do you think that will be?"

Oscar knew his moment had come. He'd been doing a little research on his own. He set the piece of chicken down on his plate before wiping his hands with the napkin. "Now, don't get mad." When he saw her head whip up, he could have kicked himself for starting that way. He held his hand up, one finger raised, before starting. "Sandy, you are doing an awesome job. I know it, you know it, your mom knows it. No one is questioning that. But it's a lot. Two babies are a lot. I'm not sure you've had more than three hours sleep at a time since they were born." He noticed that her face relaxed a bit as he continued to talk.

"Thank you. I know you're right about that."

"Now, hear me out, okay?" When she remained quiet, he continued. "I stopped by the church daycare center on my way home from work the other day. It's a small setup, about five or six infants and ten or eleven toddlers. It's cozy, not like some of the big childcare centers you see advertised. There's a good ratio of staff, plus, they're mostly people we know from church already."

"But Oscar, I don't . . ."

"Hang on now, hear me out. They don't have room for any more full-time children, but two of the babies only come Monday, Wednesday, Friday. The other two mornings, they have space. Isn't it worth thinking about, Hon? Two mornings a week to catch your breath, to catch up on chores, maybe even get ahead a bit."

"I'm not sure, Oscar. It sounds great. I know it does. I'm just not sure."

He decided to try pushing just a tiny bit more. "I wonder if maybe it wouldn't be good for your mom too? If she saw you stepping back just a bit, taking a little time for yourself, maybe she would do the same."

Sandy paused, resting her fork on the edge of the plate. "Do you think so?"

"I think it's a possibility. At least take a few days to consider it, all right? Go by there. You don't have to make any snap decisions."

Sandy picked her fork up, and Oscar was relieved to see the smile on her face. "You're a good man, Oscar, and a good dad. I'll think about it, I really will. And I'll talk to my mom too."

"Thank you, that's all I ask." They were nearly finished with their food when first one and then the other baby began to cry. When Sandy stood up and began to head into the living room, he rested his hand on her arm to stop her and kissed her on the head. "I've got them for now. You finish your dinner."

"They probably need . . ."

"I know, a change and a cuddle, and then we'll see what else they need. I'm on it." Sandy stood up on her toes and kissed him on the mouth, taking the time for a real, honest to God, married couple kiss before sitting back down at the table. For his part, Oscar began whistling a silly tune as he walked away, and the crying seemed to ebb immediately. He cast a grin back at Sandy before moving to look after his daughters.

CHAPTER

3

Audrey Markum had never attended a dog funeral, so she had no idea what to wear. She sorted slowly through the items hanging in her closet before pausing finally on a sleeveless, dark blue dress. She had worn it out to dinner once before, but she didn't think Rod was likely to remember it or even care about the repetition. For just a moment, she pictured the detective the way he looked the first afternoon that they met for coffee, Simple Simon in tow on his way home from the vet. The dog's bright, white muzzle had told her immediately of their long friendship, and she knew now that Rod was struggling with the loss. Years ago, she'd given up on owning her own car in the city, so she texted to request a car before slipping on her sandals and dabbing on a bit of lipstick. Then she gathered up her bag and went to sit on the cool, stone steps to wait.

It had been nearly three months since she'd been forced over that same threshold and across the street at gunpoint before being beaten by her captor. Her breath continued to catch whenever she stepped outside, but she hoped that the tremendous panic that had been so constant in the first few weeks after the attack had finally begun to ease. In and out, she measured her breathing as she waited for the ride. It was August in the city, and the trees planted along the street offered only a hint of shade in the stifling heat. It had been too many days since rain had fallen, and many of the leaves were beginning to develop dry, brown edges. She wished for a moment that she'd brought her camera out with her as she spotted a particularly interesting pattern in the play of sunlight, but this was not a day for taking pictures. The car arrived then, and she settled into the back seat.

Audrey smiled when she thought of the framed photograph that she had brought with her, a candid shot she'd caught of Rod leaning low, face-to-face with Simple Simon as he tried to pull a worn tennis ball from the dog's mouth. It was a photograph that she thought caught a perfect image of the joy that they had shared. On such a tough day, she hoped it would help rather than hurt.

"Hey there, Scout. Thank you so much for coming," Rod whispered in her ear as she stepped out onto the sidewalk. Audrey smiled. He'd coined the nickname well before they began dating but it had stuck, a nod to her eye for details.

She leaned in for a quick kiss. "I was happy that you included me in this." She gestured to the bag slung over her shoulder. "I brought you something."

He took her free hand in his, and they headed up the steep steps to the porch. He pulled open the front door and led her down the short hallway to the living room. "Is it going to make me cry? Because it's starting to get embarrassing."

"What's embarrassing, Uncle Rod?" asked a small boy who was wearing a tie and a straw hat while standing and bouncing on a low ottoman. Rod swept him up and dangled him over his shoulder for a second before resting him on his hip and turning toward Audrey. "Hi, I'm Far. Who are you?"

"I'm Audrey. You're Far?" Audrey asked, her head turned toward Rod as she shook the little boy's hand.

A beautiful, tall woman with the same eyes as Rod stepped forward and held out her hand to Audrey. "Franklin Avery-Rodriguez is his name. It's nice to meet you, Audrey, I'm Emma, and this is my wife, Gina." Audrey stepped forward and shook the womens' hands. She laughed as Emma told the story and pointed at the little boy who was now happily swinging back and forth in a short, upside-down arc over the ottoman, just out of reach of the hat that had fallen off. "He was supposed to be called Frank or Frankie or something normal like that, but when Uncle Rod saw his initials, that went by the wayside."

"Did you come for Simon's funeral?" the little boy asked once Rod set him back on his feet. Audrey felt the air go out of the room.

"I did." Audrey knelt in front of the boy. "I brought something for your Uncle Rod. Would you like to help him unwrap it?"

Rod sat down on a wide leather chair, then picked Far up and set him on his lap. Together they tore through the shiny blue paper to reveal the photograph. "It's him. It's Simon." Far said excitedly and then leaned against his uncle's chest. "I miss him."

Rod hugged the little boy close, but his eyes, shining just a bit, were on Audrey. "Me too, big guy. Where do you think we should put it?"

"Someplace special," his sister answered, stepping forward. She took it and centered it on the thick wooden mantle. Then she nodded at her brother, and the group headed toward the back of the house and the kitchen door that led to the yard. In Rod's neighborhood of Brookline, the houses marched up the sides of the ridges in tiered, parallel lines that followed the contour of the hillside. Rod's tier was near the top, so his lot had a pitched incline to the sidewalk in front and a small flat yard in the rear. Under a short, brushy tree, a square of earth was mounded up, a section of grass laid over the top of it.

After a brief ceremony that included a homemade cross that Far had covered with doggy stickers, the group returned inside. Gina settled Far in her lap with a book while the rest met in the kitchen and began putting together the dinner. There was a round platter of sandwiches as well as a plate of cut fruit and a plastic bowl of salad. Audrey brought the dressing bottles from the refrigerator while Emma filled glasses with ice and water. Once everything was ready, they called everyone together and sat down to eat. With a small section of sandwich held in each hand, Far turned to his Uncle Rod and asked the key question. "Are you going to get another dog?"

After the funeral dinner, Audrey and Rod sat together on his front porch, watching the wind travel through the neighborhood below them. Several people were out walking their dogs, but no one had ventured along the walk in front of his house, and Rod was silently relieved. There were lots of cars making their way up and down the steep streets, and the hot day looked to be preparing for a storm, with hints of cool air suggesting a welcome change ahead. "So, how are you doing?" Audrey asked.

Rod looked at her for a moment before responding. He blew out a long breath, not knowing what he could say that wouldn't make him sound like a blubbering half-wit. "It's hard, I feel kind of silly admitting it, but Simon was a big part of my life for a long time. Part of me knows that he had a great life, that we had a great life together, but the other part of me wants to sell the damn house because it feels so empty without him in it." He leaned forward, clasping his hands in front of him.

"And Far's question? Do you think you'll get another dog?"

Rod ran both hands through his hair, leaned back, and then reached for the beer that sat on the small table between them. "I have no idea. Right now, today, my answer is never." He shrugged. "But somewhere down the line? I just don't know." He looked at Audrey then. "With Simon gone, will it be easier for you to spend time here at my place?"

He was well aware that Audrey had grown up with a list of allergies that was a mile long and had contributed to her significant hearing loss. She reached for his hand. "I've never had any trouble when I've been here before, so I'm hoping that's one allergy I've outgrown." She gestured around her. "It's such a beautiful place. I love being here. You wouldn't really sell it, would you?"

Rod had spent years updating and refreshing the older home. He'd never had a lot of money or spare time, so his practice had been to tackle one project at a time, aiming to get it done right, if not quickly. He was proud of how the main floor looked now, but he had yet to get much done on the second floor. He shook his head as he leaned back in his chair and finished the last swallows of beer. "No, I could never sell it. I mean, the state it's in now, I literally couldn't sell it, but what I mean is, I don't actually want to sell it. I did want to get it super clean for you so you could stay over tonight," he gestured behind him in the direction of the small grave. "But I'm afraid the funeral arrangements got out of hand and cut into my cleaning time. I managed to change the sheets on the bed, but that's about as far as I got."

Audrey leaned over to kiss him, and he met her in the space between them. Then she pulled back just a bit. "I'd love to stay, but I'm due out at my folk's house in the morning. This is my last weekend without a wedding to photograph for a while, and I promised I'd spend it out at their place. They're still worried about me. Plus, I wanted to stop in and see how Sandy is doing too."

"I have to work tomorrow, but the shift doesn't start until four. Could you get a ride back into town if I drove you over in the morning?"

"Sure, if my dad can't drive me, I can use a service. Could you stay through lunch?"

"In exchange for tonight? Absolutely!" A cool wind had come up, and as the first drops of rain were starting to whip through the open porch, they headed inside. From the kitchen window, Rod could see the small mound now being pummeled by rain. He looked away and went to open the refrigerator. "You hungry?"

When he woke up in the morning, Rod's first thought was to let Simon out the back door, and he sighed deeply when the realization hit him. He sensed Audrey stirring then and wrapped his arm gently around her waist as they both closed their eyes and tried for a few more minutes of sleep. The time he and Audrey enjoyed together made it more than worth the time he spent driving out to the western suburb in the morning. Anyway, it was never a hardship hanging out with Audrey's parents. After Audrey had been assaulted, he'd rushed her out to her folks' house. Pulling up in a cop car with Audrey beaten and bloodied were terrible circumstances under which to meet, but he'd made a helluva first impression on them, and they'd welcomed him ever since.

The two of them arrived at mid-morning, and after sitting and visiting for a while, he and Audrey headed over to her friend Sandy's house. The twins Rose and Martha had been born the day before Audrey's ordeal had begun, so Rod had a hard time not associating the two events. Terror and joy in the space of one weekend. How did people cope with the sheer oddness of life, he wondered?

"Rosey, my love, how are you?" Audrey cooed as she lifted the child in her arms and then nuzzled her neck for a small kiss.

"How does she do that?" Oscar stood rocking Martha gently in his arms while Sandy brought them each some iced tea. He held up the baby's foot and pointed it toward Rod. "See that freckle? I still have to double-check for the damned thing to be sure I've got the right one. She just walks right in and knows!"

Rod loved the sound of Audrey's laugh. "You know you can't put anything over on Scout, don't you? She's got the eye."

"Creepy, huh?" Oscar asked, winking at Rod as he did it.

"I am not creepy, you jerks. I just know Rosey better, that's all. When she first came home, and I was healing, we spent time together."

"That's right," Sandy added as she took a seat on the couch. "Rosey cried so much at first, remember? Audrey was the only one who managed to keep smiling while she rocked her over and over."

"Yup," Audrey gestured at the hearing aid in her right ear. "Just put these bad boys in their case, and I was good to go. Now though," she shrugged. "I can't put my finger on how I know the difference. Sometimes I think maybe you recognize a twin by the way they look back at you."

Oscar gently shifted Martha into Rod's hands and watched. Rod knew he was supposed to half-panic, but he'd looked after Far enough to know his way around a baby. "Hello, sweetheart." He rubbed his finger across her cheek and watched as her gaze shifted around her. "What's she looking for?"

Audrey stepped closer and watched as the two infants locked gazes. "I think she's looking for her sister."

Sandy nodded. "It's a little spooky sometimes. I have to say. They are way more focused on each other than they are on any of us. I've been reading up on twins lately. We never had any in our family before." She gestured toward her husband. "He's got a couple of twin cousins, but my side has none."

Oscar reached his arm around Sandy. "I never knew them until they were adults going their separate ways so, pshh. We've got nothing to go on."

"Well, I think it's sweet," Audrey added. "Since I'm an only child, I can't imagine what it would be like to grow up with a twin, but I'm pretty sure it would be amazing."

No one could argue with that, Rod thought, as the conversation shifted around to other topics. In a little while, it was time for lunch and then the trip back into the city. He lifted an eyebrow at Audrey, and she recognized the signal that they'd agreed on. She certainly did have the eye, he thought and smiled as he handed Martha back over to Oscar.

"What's your name, darlin'?" Julius smiled at the young waitress setting the tall pint down on the bar in front of him. She had a sweet face and didn't seem put off at all by his approach. He smoothed the hair down along the back of his head and straightened his collar.

"I'm Mia. And you are?"

"Julius." He put out his hand, and she shook it casually as she lifted her tray with the other.

"Nice to meet you, Julius. Can I get you anything else?"

He tilted the bowl of peanuts that he'd just emptied. "Got any more of these?"

"Of course!" The bar was still relatively empty, and he watched as Mia first filled his bowl and then several more, setting them down at intervals along the length of the bar. He continued to watch as she chatted with the two other groups, a young couple drinking sodas and looking out of place and a pair of laborers, construction, he thought, given the light coating of dust that both of them were covered in. Then, she worked her way back around the room and behind the bar.

Julius knew he shouldn't have taken the time to stop in. Hannah would be waiting for him, but his meeting had wrapped up early, and he couldn't bear to head home sooner than was absolutely necessary. It was just past three, and as he looked around him, he thought it would probably be a few hours before the place picked up. He wondered if Mia might have time for more of a chat and was happy when she obliged, perching comfortably on the barstool beside his. "So, I don't think I've seen you working here before. Are you new?"

She spun a stirring stick in a lazy circle on the bar top. "Yeah, my cousin owns this bar, and he heard I was trying to make a little more money, so he gave me some afternoon hours. Mornings, I work in a day-care center. I thought about going back to school, trying to get a degree in it or something, but daycare doesn't pay shit."

"Would you study something else then?"

"Not sure yet, but yeah, maybe. My friend is taking business classes at the community college, and she keeps telling me I should join her. We have some ideas for starting our own business someday."

"That sounds great." He sipped at his beer and watched as her eyes scanned the room before settling back on him. He took the chance and rested his hand lightly on her knee. When she didn't seem to object, his shoulders relaxed, and a smile spread slowly across his face. He'd stepped out on Hannah a few times before, but it had been a while. Now, he was especially glad that his meeting had ended early.

Once lunch with her parents was finished, and Audrey had seen Rod off, she walked back over to Sandy's to visit a little more and to see if she might be able to help. Her mother and father had been heading over to a friend's for the afternoon, so Audrey was hoping to make herself useful while they were gone. Sandy still had that exhausted, new mother look to her eyes, and it worried her.

Audrey knocked quietly before letting herself in through the kitchen door as she had as a child. She could hear a TV in the back den but found Sandy alone in the living room in front of two baskets that each held a minor mountain of clean laundry. "Oh my God, what is this?" Audrey plopped down beside her friend and grabbed a onesie to fold.

"This, my dear, is just three days' worth, if you can believe it. You have no idea how many times a day we have to change their clothes. And this is in the summer! I'm already dreading what the laundry will look like this fall. Our water bill will be through the roof."

"So, where is everybody?" Audrey asked as she continued to help fold the tiny outfits and stack them into piles. It seemed as though more than half of the outfits were either purple or green, so she automatically sorted them accordingly.

"Oh, the girls are upstairs sleeping, and my mom's down in the den watching the game. Oscar wanted to mow, but I was afraid it would wake the babies, so he's gone to the grocery and hardware store instead." Sandy let her hands drop into her lap for a moment. "Can I ask you a question?"

"Sure, anything."

"Oscar has this crazy idea that we should put the girls in daycare two mornings a week."

"What's crazy about that? I love you, but you look fairly exhausted to me. Wouldn't that help?"

Sandy dumped one basket onto the couch between them and then began moving the stacks of folded clothes into it. "I just feel so guilty even thinking about it."

"But why? Can you afford it?"

"We can. Oscar stopped into the place at our church and got all of the details. I know for sure we'll have to do some daycare when I go back to work. I'll mostly be remote, but there will still be times when I have to go into the law office. I just wasn't ready to face it yet."

"I'm guessing you can't leave them with your mom, right?'

Sandy shook her head. "No, and that's part of Oscar's reasoning. Mom needs to have her knees replaced. She's in so much pain. He thinks she's putting it off until I'm on my feet better, that this would show her that we're managing."

"Well, I'm probably the last person you should be asking since I have zero experience in this area. But, if you think someone's going to be judging you or thinking less of you and Oscar for having a little help, then forget it. Every marriage, every family, has to figure things out for themselves. You and Oscar will get there. I know it." Audrey gestured at the basket now filled with the neatly folded little outfits. "Can I ask, what's up with all the purple and green?" It was nice to hear Sandy's quick laugh.

"Unlike you, my dear, most ordinary humans have a bit of trouble telling the girls apart, so for a while at least, Martha is going to be green girl, and Rosey will be purple. I figure once they're older, they can fight it out for themselves. Besides, if we end up putting them in daycare, it will help everyone keep them straight."

A shrill wail echoed through the air, and Sandy rose, the filled laundry basket tucked under her arm. She took Audrey by the other arm and led her toward the stairs. A second cry added to the first. "Come with me, my dear. If they've pooped and managed to get it all over the crib again, you'll see the real joys of motherhood up close and personal."

Audrey hesitated a fraction of a second, long enough to register a look of horror on her face, before following her friend up the stairs to whatever was waiting for them.

6

Rod was glad to see his partner Smitty back in the office, but disappointed that he'd not been returned to the homicide division yet. Just before Audrey's ordeal, Smitty had taken a bullet in the gut when a team went after some rednecks who'd shot up a dance club. The recovery had taken longer than anyone had liked, especially Smitty. Rod stood in front of what he hoped would be his friend's temporary desk, both hands held behind his back. "Which hand, partner? You feeling lucky?"

"What the hell are you doing?" Smitty asked, pointing at Rod's left arm but also edging back a bit in his seat.

"It's your lucky day!" Rod brought out a chocolate pudding cup and set it on the desk in front of his partner.

"What is this shit, Goddamnit? You know I'm sick to death of those things. What kind of asshole are you?"

Rod slowly brought his other hand forward, revealing a bright green jello cup. "Not in the mood for pudding then?"

Smitty bent over laughing but gestured wildly at the two snacks. "Get that shit away from me if you have any interest in living." Rod pulled two plastic spoons from his back pocket and proceeded to open the pudding. "Oh God, gimme that shit." Smitty laughed and swapped the jello for the pudding. "Do not tell my wife that I'm eating this. Do you hear me?"

Rod put half of the jello in his mouth before nodding. "It's good to have you back, my friend, good to have you back. I wish you were sitting down the hall with me, but . . ."

"I know, missing persons sucks, but until I can re-qualify, they're not going to put me back out there. What have you got going on right now?"

"Nothing much, a drug buy went bad north of the river, and a kid was hit in the crossfire. Shooter was only sixteen." Rod dropped the empty jello container in the trash. "The DA is already talking about trying him as an adult."

"But you got your guy, right?"

"Yep, he's bawling his eyes out in 3B." Rod shook his head with the waste of it all before looking up again at his partner. "You hit anything interesting yet?"

"Hell no, I just sat down. Of course not."

"Well, if there's anything I can do, let me know. I'll be just down the hall doing the important work if you need me!"

Rod was happy to see Smitty looking as good as he did, especially after what he'd been through, but it didn't make him any more eager to return to his desk. The shooter's parents were due in less than an hour. He hoped to God they were able to afford a halfway decent attorney for the kid. He fucking hated cases like this where absolutely everyone lost. The shooter was probably as much of a victim as the kid he killed. No way he had the kind of money that was behind the drug deal. Some fat cat sitting uptown in front of a fancy computer was the one at fault, but no one would be touching him. Not now, probably not ever. It all sucked.

It was after six before the kid was transferred, and his parents headed home. It was all out of his hands now, for better or worse, and there was nothing left to do but head home himself. Rod didn't even have a dog waiting for him anymore. He knew Audrey had been busy photographing a wedding all weekend, but he hoped she might be free to get together tonight. He'd pick up a couple of steaks and see if she'd like to come over and grill out. A good meal and the sight of Audrey would definitely help to balance out the crappy day.

He was sitting on his front porch with a beer when she stepped out of the car. He watched as she entered a tip on her phone and then pulled an enormous bag over her shoulder. He stood up quickly and went to meet her. "What's all this?"

"Hey there!" She stood on her tiptoes to meet his kiss. "It's a salad for dinner and some egg rolls that my friend Katy made." Audrey tipped her head from side to side, "Uh, also my laptop and a few things for overnight, just in case."

He grinned. "I love just in case. C'mon in." He carried Audrey's bag in and set it on the counter in the kitchen. She lifted out the food she'd brought while he loaded up a tray with the steaks, a clean plate, long-handled tongs, and the rest of his beer. "There's beer if you like, and I picked up some soda. I got some great potato salad from the deli, too. It's in a green bowl if you don't mind grabbing it."

Rod's back porch looked out over the small backyard that was overgrown just enough to feel cozy and private. He noticed that Simon's mound had sunk considerably, and Far's homemade cross was starting to lean just a bit, but he put it out of mind. While the grill heated, they sampled the egg rolls and set up the table. They'd started to develop a little bit of a rhythm, Rod thought, and that seemed to make up for the lousy day even more.

Once everything was set, Audrey propped her feet up on the railing and watched as Rod set the steaks on the hot grill. "So, spill it, chief. What's up?"

He hooked the tongs on the side of the grill and looked over at her. "How do you know something's up, Scout?"

"I know Smitty was due back. Is he okay?"

Rod took the seat beside her and leaned in for a quick kiss. "Yep, he's good. He needs to put some weight back on, but that's going to take time. It's great having him back."

"But . . ."

"You're right. It was a shitty kind of day, kids shooting kids. I'm glad you weren't called in."

As Audrey continued to build her wedding photography business, she worked part-time as a police photographer to help make ends meet. "I thought dumpster diving was the worst." She shook her head. "I'm sorry I was wrong. I'm back on call starting tomorrow."

"We're hoping it was a one-off, but you never know. Now let's change the subject. How was your wedding?"

They chatted easily as Rod lifted the steaks off the grill and settled them on the extra plate before retrieving the tall bottle of ketchup from inside. Audrey gawked as he poured out a substantial puddle. "Hey, don't judge me, okay?" He went back inside, and this time brought out a beautiful tomato and a serrated knife and handed them both to Audrey. "We just like our tomato in different formats, is all." He knew Audrey was one of those people who raved on and on about tomatoes in the summertime, but he'd never really seen the appeal. Still, he happily bought them for her.

"Thank you, sir. The wedding went well. There was an uncle that got pretty drunk and handsy, but they handled it. The venue was one I'd been at before, so that made it easy. Oh," She rested the knife on the edge of the plate before turning to look up at Rod. "I talked with Sandy on the way over here. The first couple of weeks with the girls going to daycare went okay. She said it was a contest who was crying more, her or Oscar, but they made it through. She picked them up a half-hour early on Tuesday but managed to wait until noon on Thursday, so she counted it as progress."

"So, it's a big deal to leave them for a few hours?"

"Yep, I think it's scary for them. But Sandy's mom did agree to meet with the orthopedic surgeon next week, so that counts as progress too, I suppose."

They took their time with dinner, finally settling into the living room with their dueling laptops. Rod knew she was probably working, but he was just enjoying having her near, fiddling around looking at box scores from the weekend and updating his fantasy league. It was an excellent way to end a crappy day, he thought, and reached a hand over to rub the side of her leg. When she closed the lid on her laptop fifteen minutes later, he figured it was about to get even better.

Once she was back at her apartment, Audrey's busy week got started in earnest. Most of Tuesday morning was taken up with photographing a messy crime scene at a drugstore. A young addict had gone crazy, first threatening the pharmacist, then holding a frail, older woman hostage before tossing her to the floor and bashing the displays apart with an aluminum bat. Luckily, he had collapsed in frustration on the floor rather than taking the baseball bat to any of the bystanders. Still, the drugstore manager had wanted a thorough photographic record of the damage, and it had taken Audrey quite a while.

Once she was back at the precinct, Audrey took her time wrapping everything up and stowing the gear. She had hoped for a glimpse of Rod before she left, but he'd been called out before she arrived. Reluctantly, she shouldered her bag and headed for the bus stop that would take her back downtown and her appointment with the city attorney who was handling her attacker's prosecution. Those meetings were never fun since they always seemed to involve rehashing everything that had happened to her in the attack without ever really moving forward. She hoped that today would be different.

Audrey had met Gabriel Perez, an attorney for the city of Pittsburgh, in the spring. His mother and father were housekeeper and gardener for a wealthy, older woman who had died in a fall, and Audrey had met Gabriel when she was photographing the scene. He had stepped in to comfort his parents and make sure that they were treated fairly throughout the police investigation. In the end, the woman's death was declared an accident, and his parents continued to live and work at the beautiful home.

After Audrey was assaulted and began having to navigate the many steps that followed, she was pleased to see a face that she recognized. She'd felt comfortable with Gabriel's forthright approach and steady supply of information.

"Audrey, come in. Have a seat." Gabriel shook her hand and ushered her into one of the worn chairs that sat facing his broad desk. He shared the office with three other attorneys for the city, each encamped in a different corner of the large room. "Can I get you something to drink?"

"No thanks, I'm good, just anxious to hear the latest." Audrey thought that the thick file folder that lay open in front of him was even larger than it had been the last time she'd been in.

"I know, it can feel as though this process takes forever, but we are moving steadily through the steps. I'd been waiting for the outcome of the pretrial conference before I called you."

"Can you explain to me again what that is?"

"Sure, the pretrial conference is a big step. It's where the defendant's lawyer hears the evidence that we'll be presenting as well as the list of witnesses."

"They get to know all of that ahead of time?" Audrey sank back into the chair, frustrated again at the entire ordeal.

"Yes, it's called Discovery, and it's required in order for a trial to be fair. We laid out the information that we have about him subletting the apartment across from yours, for example, and the materials that we found in his car."

"Is that all we have? It doesn't sound like very much." Audrey had first seen her attacker when she was a child and found the buried body of his son, her friend Toby. Twenty years after that, as soon as he'd been released from prison, he'd come after her. Now Audrey paled at the thought of having to face Gary Adams once again.

Gabriel picked up the thick file in front of him and shook his head. "No, Audrey, that's not all we have, and you know it."

"Okay, I know I'm being a whiner here." She sat up straighter in her chair and leaned toward the young attorney. "Go ahead."

"All right, so the other thing that happens at the pretrial conference is a discussion of any deals."

"I know you told me that your office was considering a plea deal; did he take it?"

"That's what I wanted to tell you about today. Our office did offer to reduce the charges from Attempted Murder to Aggravated Assault with a minimum sentence of 15 years."

"That makes my skin crawl, you know, the idea of seeing him out again so soon." Audrey clasped her hands together in her lap and waited for him to continue.

"I know, I didn't much like the idea myself. But, as it turns out, Adams didn't like the idea either. He rejected the offer."

"Why would he do that? I don't understand."

"Well," Gabriel leaned back in his seat. "Apparently, Mr. Adams thinks he's smarter than his court-appointed lawyer, and he'd rather go to trial. So, the charges have been officially entered, Attempted Murder-first degree for his assault on you, and Aggravated Assault for the shots he took at the policemen before he was captured. He's pleading Not Guilty to both, so it looks like we're going to trial after all."

"Oh God, that's going to be awful, isn't it? Will people hear about him murdering his son and the fact that I found the body?"

"No, unfortunately not. That information was all ruled inadmissible."

"Why? It's the reason he came after me. He told me so."

"I realize that, but when someone's on trial for a crime similar to one they were already convicted for, it's considered prejudicial to mention the earlier offense."

"So, people are supposed to think I'm just some random woman he stalked and attacked? That doesn't make any sense."

"Trials can be unwieldy things, so what we have to do is narrow our focus. We have evidence of his planning to capture you, evidence of the harm Adams caused you, and we have the police officers who witnessed him shooting at them. It's a strong case, Audrey. We would have pushed harder for a deal if we didn't think we had what we needed to convict him."

Audrey let her breath out in a whoosh and spread her hands out on her knees, flexing them to restore the blood flow. "All right, I understand what you're saying. So, what happens next?"

"The homicide rate in the city has been going down, and folks in city government like that trend. They want to see this trial wrapped up quickly. We're going to start jury selection this week. Then you can expect things to kick into high gear."

"Okay, so in the meantime? Am I supposed to be doing anything?"

Gabriel stood and came around to sit on the front of the desk. "Audrey, you don't have to do a thing. This is my job now to get everything ready and to keep you informed as we move forward. Your job is just to keep healing. How are you doing anyway?"

Audrey stood as well. "I'm better, physically all better. The nerves," she wiggled her hand in front of her, "I guess they're still a little jangly."

"Well, keep in mind, we have services available for victims if you need them."

She shook his hand again, noticing the long, slim fingers and the thin gold wedding band. "Thanks, I'm lucky that I have my family and friends to lean on."

"And a certain police detective, I hear?" Audrey laughed. "You know, I liked Detective Rodriguez when I met him in the spring. He was good with my folks, treated them with respect as well as kindness. But," he paused, and Audrey looked at his face. "Don't underestimate the value of counseling. It can make a real difference. I know. I've seen it help."

"Thank you, Gabriel. I'll keep it in mind. I've got the number for victims' services that you gave me."

He moved them toward the door. "All right. You take care now. I'll be in touch."

"I will, Gabriel, and thank you again for everything.

"So why does your wife want a baby so bad?"

Julius closed his eyes briefly and leaned his head back against the pillow. He put so much effort into keeping his world divided into neat compartments that he hated to even think about his wife when Mia was right there in front of him. He traced the lines of the wide butterfly tattoo up and around her beautiful little breasts. "Because she can't have any, I guess. Isn't that what always makes us want things?"

"I don't know, we just had twins start at the daycare, and the parents look like hammered shit. I figure they must be pretty sick of them already."

He watched as the young woman stretched her hand out for the cigarette that was smoldering beside the bed. Its smoke was slowly replacing the sweeter scent of the weed that they'd had earlier, and he wished she'd put it out. He took it from her, enjoyed a long pull on it, and then snuffed it out in the messy glass bowl beside the small lamp.

"Hey, I wasn't done with that," she objected.

"Sure, you were, sugar." He pulled her over on top of him and felt the excitement rebuilding. It was nice to know he wasn't as old as he'd been feeling lately. Once they'd finished again, he sat up and began pulling on his clothes. He'd seen the pitiful excuse for a spray from Mia's shower and the wall of products she and her roommate had accumulated. He had no desire to fight his way through any of that, so he thought he'd stop by his gym on the way home and grab a quick shower. Maybe his wife would meet him for dinner somewhere. God knew he didn't need to ruin the great afternoon he'd had with one of his wife's new organic dinner experiments.

He liked that Mia wasn't clingy at all, and it was a quick walk to his gym from her place. He turned the water as hot as he could stand it and then allowed it to rush down his back, easing out the kinks from a day at his desk. He started to get hard again as he pictured Mia and her tattoo, but those thoughts were pushed aside as he began to think back over what she'd said. Twins, who in the world would want to have to manage two babies at the same time? He'd read all about fertility treatments and knew that multiples were way more common now that in vitro was becoming so popular, but that hadn't been an option for Hannah, and secretly he'd been relieved. Maybe the ragged-out couple that had the twins didn't even want two babies. He'd have to give it a bit more thought, but a plan might be forming, and Mia would be the perfect partner for it.

Oscar slung one diaper bag over each shoulder before hefting a car seat up with each hand. Getting the babies to daycare in the morning was an elaborate process, but he thought maybe he was starting to get the hang of it. He was so pleased that both Sandy and her mother were looking better. It made all of the work worthwhile. "Okay, my little green dumpling." He spoke as he nuzzled Martha's sweet-smelling neck and then fastened her seat into place. The green bag went at her feet. He repeated the process with Rosey and was relieved that neither had set up a cry. He waved at Sandy in the doorway and was off.

The ride to the church was quick, and he pulled up into the circular drive that led to the back door. He removed one carrier seat and bag and brought them around to the side of the car before repeating the process. Luckily there was a handicap button for the two sets of wide doors, so he was in quickly with his double load.

"Good morning, Mr. Wilder-Smith." Mia, the young helper, greeted him at the door and took the two diaper bags to store in the cubbies. Although he and Sandy had talked a great deal with the director, Miriam Bianchi, initially, it was the young assistant that they seemed to end up interacting with the most. Together she and Oscar unstrapped both infants and carried them over to a soft fleece blanket that lay spread out on the carpet along with a scattering of baby toys.

"Please, it's just Oscar."

The young woman beamed a warm smile at him. "Okay, Oscar, we've got this."

He bent low to kiss each of the girls before straightening and heading for the door. "My wife will be here for them at noon." He added a short wave and was off.

As he left, Mia studied the room they were in, just as Julius had asked her to. They were in a wing of the main church building, one that spread down to the left away from the sanctuary so that cries wouldn't be heard during services. There were six rooms altogether, three on each side, with connecting doors in between. The daycare took up just the left-hand side. Infants were in the first room, the cots, cribs, and changing tables in the middle room, and the toddler area was on the far end. Mia noted the number of entrances and exits on a small notepad that Julius had given her, but she had found it easier to draw a little map of the place than write it all down in detail. In the bathroom for a brief moment, she spread her map out and used two colored pencils to indicate where the twin babies were during the morning. That was enough for now. The last thing he wanted to know was about fire alarms and sprinklers, but that would take more looking around than she had time for now.

At first, Mia had been reluctant to even consider Julius's idea about taking one of the twin girls. She loved being with him though, and was always wishing he'd stay longer instead of rushing home to his wife. Julius had suggested that if his wife was happy at home dealing with the baby, he and Mia might have even more time together. She had remained hesitant however, until he mentioned the money. He'd offered her a big lump sum or, a set amount a month and she'd like the idea of that even better. It would be enough that she could afford a place of her own. No more cranky roommates and more privacy for the two of them. There was still time to think about the whole idea, though, as she went around collecting the information that she would need if they went through with it. With her mind settled once again, she folded the paper carefully and slid it into her pocket, then washed her hands and went back into the infant room.

"Not again," she moaned. Rosey, the twin in purple, was already crying. What was it with her? Everything was obviously fine, her sister was happily playing with a squeaky teething toy, but no, this one was busy crying her head off again. The older woman had been walking her around while Mia was in the bathroom, but she quickly handed her over and turned to sit on the blanket with the happier, contented infants. It figured, Mia thought, as she went to find a tissue to control some of the snot that was bound to get all over her. For the millionth time, she decided that she really needed a new job. Daycare work didn't pay shit. Or, it paid *in* shit, if she was right about what she was smelling. Give her a bar and a bunch of fat drunks any day, she thought as she carried the baby into the changing room next door.

Hours later, Mia was glad to be carrying the two diaper bags and following Mrs. Wilder-Smith to her car. The woman kept on fawning over the babies as she fastened them into their car seats, and it was starting to make Mia feel a little bit queasy. Even though there were two of them, and the purple one was a crying machine, the mother still seemed awfully attached to both infants. Mia wasn't quite so sure that Julius's assessment of the situation was correct.

10

Katy Huang was a beauty, Audrey thought, as she focused her lens one more time. They had met as college freshmen, but Audrey had to admit that they'd become better friends once they were no longer living together. Katy was a musician, the newest cellist in Pittsburgh's celebrated symphony. But Audrey knew that the cello was just a gateway instrument for Katy as their dorm room had slowly filled with an assortment of guitars, amps, and a number of odd flutes. The clutter and the sheer volume associated with it had nearly done Audrey in. Now, Audrey grinned as she motioned for Katy and her fiancé Brian to sit on the bench. "We're getting married," Katy gushed. "This is so exciting!" Audrey laughed at her friend's exuberance and tried to capture it in the photos. It wasn't hard to do since it seemed to leak out of the two of them like water.

"Okay, guys, I think we're done." Audrey watched as Brian sagged back against the rough seat. They were on one of the paved paths down near the waterfront as a gaudy, touristy riverboat motored its way down the river behind them. Audrey had worked quickly and was happy that she had managed *not* to include it in the engagement shots. "It's official. I'll send you the file tonight so that you can upload them to your wedding website."

Katy looked at Brian before turning back to Audrey. "I still can't quite believe it's happening, and in less than two months!"

Brian grabbed her hand, and the two of them up stood up. "I'm glad it's coming soon, aren't you?"

Katy leaned in for a kiss before nodding her head in agreement. "Yup, the sooner, the better." She turned to Audrey then, her expression moving into regret. "I'm still so sorry that I can't have you in the wedding party with me, Audrey. It sucks having sisters."

"No, it doesn't, you idiot. I think it would be great to have sisters, and you know I'm happy and honored to be the one doing the photography." Audrey packed up her camera bag, and the three of them headed down the path, back toward the downtown area where they were planning to have dinner. The couple was a tad overdressed for the casual bar and grill, but no one cared, least of all them.

In a reasonably short time, they settled into a deep red booth with their drinks and a basket of house-made chips. Katy leaned forward. "So, what's the scoop on the hot detective? Have you done it in a police car yet?"

"Katy!" Brian dropped his head into his hands. "My God . . ."

"What?" She looked up in surprise as Audrey began to laugh.

"No boundaries. The woman has no boundaries whatsoever." Brian shook his head and reached for another chip.

"It's fine, Brian. I'm used to it. After I went out for the first time my freshman year, she asked me what my date's dick looked like." Brian choked on his drink as Katy leaned back in the booth, waving her hand in dismissal.

"I just like to know these things, these details." She paused. "So, have you?"

"First, no, because once you're out of high school who wants to do it in a car, and second, he doesn't usually drive a cop car. He's a detective."

"Oh well, I guess that makes sense." She looked over at her husband-to-be. "All right, I get it, safer topic. How's your friend Sandy doing with her twins? They're what, almost four months by now?"

"Yep, you're right. They're pretty good. Sandy and Oscar are exhaust-ed, of course, but the girls have started at a daycare a couple of mornings a week so that everyone can catch their breath."

Brian had a frightened look on his face as he leaned back suddenly in his seat. "My God, can you imagine two babies at the same time? I could not handle that!"

Katy turned and looked at him, one eyebrow raised quizzically. "You do know that I'm a twin, right, and that they tend to run in families?"

"Oh man, I forgot! Holy shit, what will we do?"

Audrey reached across the table to rest her hand on his forearm. "You will cope, and you will lean on your friends, just like everyone else."

"Plus," Katy added. "We agreed that we're not starting a family right away, correct, even if both of our families start the full-court press? Isn't that what we said?"

Audrey knew that Katy's musical career was just getting started, and she was relieved to see Brian smiling back at her friend, a look of ease returning to his face. "That is exactly our plan."

Audrey had been thinking more about twins lately. Now that the conversation had shifted out of the danger zone, she asked. "Katy, are you and your twin sister very much alike?"

Katy fished a broken chip out of the dip before reaching for a napkin. "In some ways, I think. We looked a lot more alike as little kids than we do now that we're older."

"Matching outfits, that sort of thing?"

"Yes, and haircuts and shoes, but in elementary, we got interested in playing different instruments and different sports, so the gap widened. Are Sandy's little girls a lot alike?"

"Well," Audrey tipped her head to the side, "I can tell them apart, but that's not true for everyone. They've got different, color-coded outfits, so that helps. Plus, although Martha's a real pearl, sweet and easy-going, Rosey just got the official colic diagnosis, so she's more of a challenge." Audrey paused. "It's funny, though."

"What?" Katy asked.

"Whenever you lay them down in the crib together, Martha always searches for Rosey's hand or foot or whatever she can hold on to. It's al-most like she's looking after her. They're trying to decide if Rosey's crying means they should put them in separate cribs more often, but they're having a hard time deciding." She held her palms up like a scale. "Pluses and minuses both ways."

Their talk shifted away from twins and babies to more general topics that interested them all, including Katy's upcoming concert series and the opening of football season. Brian leaned forward suddenly. "Hey, I saw your photo! The one you took of the couple with the Steeler's wedding. It was awesome!" He turned toward Katy with his mouth open as if he had suddenly had a great idea, but she shut him down immediately.

"No way, ever!"

"I know, but still, it was cool."

"Where did you see it?" Katy asked.

"That's so great that you noticed it, Brian!" Audrey turned to Katy. "The PR department from the stadium used the photo in a big pre-season flier that they did. But really, it was because of the setting and that the couple was semi-famous, not because of me."

"But you got paid, right?" Katy wiped her mouth and pushed her plate out of the way.

"I did, a pretty fair amount. But even better, they included my website in the credits, and it's generated a bunch of hits. I never knew so many people wanted sports-themed weddings. I hope I don't end up having to specialize in them just to make money!"

"How is business?" Brian asked.

"It's good, growing, not enough to give up the police gig yet but maybe someday. My secret dream is that someone will hire me to photograph their destination wedding. Can you say 'all-expense-paid trip' to Maui, maybe? Then I'll know I've arrived. Until then?" She shrugged. "The crime and mayhem keep the lights on. What can I say?"

Katy shivered. "Do not say anything more. Ugh! I don't know how you do it. Should we head out?" Brian covered the dinner, and Audrey added a generous tip, and they were on their way in just a few minutes. The night was still warm and close when they walked to the bus stand. Audrey found herself remembering that late summer night when she'd first gone out with the police department. They'd brought in the body of a man who had drowned, and Audrey had been so overwhelmed she'd considered changing jobs that very night. But now, when she looked back, she was glad she had stuck with it. She knew that taking those kinds of detailed photographs helped to keep her skills sharp. Plus, if it hadn't been for the police work, she would never have met Rod. There was a sense of balance, Audrey thought, and that she valued very highly.

11

Julius punched the bed pillow into shape before shoving it behind him as he leaned back against the headboard. Mia was smoking another one of her cigarettes, but he tried to ignore it. "This is outstanding work, babe." He was staring at the detailed map that she had put together of the daycare center.

She reached over to point, moving her finger from room to room. "These are the locations of sprinkler heads, and these are the smoke detectors."

"I've been reading up on these systems, the rules to make code and stuff. I was hoping we could use them as a diversion, but it turns out they're tough to set off, not like in the movies. We'll need something else. What's the busiest time you can think of when people are the most distracted?"

Mia stubbed out the end of her cigarette and reached in the pack for more, but when she discovered it was empty, she just tossed it toward the trashcan and then slid over closer to Julius in bed. "I don't know really, it's a small place, pretty quiet usually. It's a little bit busy when they're feeding the toddlers their lunch. Something is always getting spilled, and they often ask one of us to come over and help. But the only crazy time I can remember was when we had a fire drill a few months ago. Our director said the city is getting stricter about them, but we fucked that one up big time. The alarm on one of the doors kept blaring, and no one knew how to turn it off. The cribs are all on wheels, but it turns out you can't get them through the doorways or anything, so we just started grabbing up the babies and a few blankets. The toddlers were all crying because there wasn't time to put on their coats, and it was a cold morning."

"And now? Are there more planned?"

She took a sip from the cold cup of coffee sitting on her nightstand. Julius marveled that she didn't even blink at the bitterness of it, especially since he figured it had probably been sitting there for at least a day. "There's one coming up. I'm pretty sure. We haven't practiced anything, but someone did make up a bunch of new signs. The director probably knows when it'll be. I imagine they'll want to do it while it's still warm outside. It's just easier that way."

"Do you think you could find out when it's going to be?"

She took the map from him and indicated a desk area drawn in along the back wall. "That's Mrs. Bianchi's desk. She has a calendar that she keeps in a drawer, but I might be able to get a look at it." She set the map back on the nightstand and turned to face him. "Even if we figure this plan out, and I'm still not sure if I'm sold on it, I don't understand how you're going to explain a baby to your wife."

He could sense that the idea of sneaking around was both frightening and exciting to Mia and he had no doubt that he'd be able to convince her to see it through for him, for them. She was smart to hesitate though, and he knew he needed to allow her time to come around to the idea. He leaned in and began stroking her long, blonde hair, looping a thick strand around her face and tickling her chin with the end of it. "I'll just tell her that the adoption agency reached out to me at work. I expect she'll be so over the moon that she won't think much about the logistics of it." He leaned in to kiss Mia then, catching her lower lip before releasing her. "You are so good to me, love. I don't know what to say."

She had a pretend pout on her face as she leaned in as well. "Say you'll stay a bit longer? Please?"

He didn't have the time, but he grabbed her up quickly and wrapped both hands around her bottom. "I think I can stay a little longer."

Twenty minutes later, he was in his car, nearly home. He knew that Hannah would be late that evening. Her license was coming up for renewal, and she had not kept up with the required continuing education credits. The month before, when she mentioned that she was about to sign up for a bunch of online classes, he'd stepped in and persuaded her to choose the ones offered at the community college building instead.

He'd reasoned that anything to get her out of the damned house, to get her mind off babies even for the briefest of moments, would be good for her. Plus, it had given him more opportunities to be with Mia and for that he was particularly grateful.

As he stepped into the bedroom and began collecting things for a shower, he thought back over their conversation about the daycare center. Julius thought that he needed to play up the idea of the money and Mia having her own place a little more. He could understand her hesitancy but the more he thought about it, the more he became convinced that they could pull it off. Years ago, with his mother's warnings about Hannah still ringing in his ears, Julius had taken a bit of her advice to heart and set up his own, separate finances. It helped that Hannah had inherited money from her parents and hadn't minded the separation. Although it wasn't easy hiding money from an accountant, Julius had listened to the tips she'd been giving clients over the years, and he had grown his account considerably. Now, he had enough to help Mia with a place of her own and get Hannah the baby she needed. With perfect timing, he stepped out of the bathroom freshly showered and was tying the belt to his robe when Hannah walked in. "How did it go?"

She dropped her bag on the nearest chair and kicked off her sandals. "It was fine. They're all morons, but it's okay. Only two more sessions. Did you get dinner?"

"Yep. I'm good. Can I get you anything to eat?" He started toward her, thinking maybe they could sit down on the couch together for a little while before bed, but instead, she walked immediately to her computer and began looking at her email. He knew that once again, there would be nothing from any of the adoption agencies, once again, she would start to tear up, and he, in turn, would leave the room. It had become all too familiar a routine. He went by and kissed her on the top of her head, holding her shoulders briefly before walking into the kitchen to pour himself a quick drink. He downed it in one gulp and then headed for the bedroom. Setting thoughts of Hannah aside, he pictured Mia's bright tattoo winding its way so carefully around her breasts and down to her navel. He slipped into the bed and shut off the light, hoping he might dream of it.

Thursday morning, Mia met the twins' father Oscar at the door and took the two diaper bags from him, pushing each one into its designated cubby. Once he was gone and she was sitting on the floor with four of the infants spread out on the soft blanket, she rested her hand on sweet little Martha's back and thought about the plan. Julius had forced them to review it so many times she'd gotten angry, but now that the day was here, she found that the extra practice was helping with her jitters. Just stick to the plan, she told herself, just stick to the plan. When Martha reached for a toy that was just beyond her, Mia picked up both the baby and the toy and cuddled the infant in her lap. She looked across the blanket and could see that Rosey was starting up a wail, so she stood and took Martha with her to the changing room, calling over her shoulder to the other young assistant. "I've got this one." She scrunched her nose as if there was a smelly diaper involved.

One of the things that Mia liked about baby Martha was that she always seemed so damn happy, especially compared to her sister. Mia laid the baby down on the changing table and pulled the green diaper bag open. She was reaching in for a clean diaper when she spotted the cap to a fat tube of sunscreen. She pulled the bag open wider and found that the sunscreen had gone everywhere. It looked as though every item in the bag was covered in the slick, greasy cream. Mia salvaged a diaper from an outside compartment and turned to change the baby, but while she had been studying the bag, Martha had delivered an unexpected load to the current diaper. Brown, greasy strands of poop were oozing out everywhere, around the fitted legs of the onesie and onto the blue changing pad. "Goddamit," Mia muttered under her breath.

Carefully, she peeled away the cloth outfit and the filthy diaper and, with at least half a container of baby wipes, slowly got the situation under control. Naked but for the clean diaper, Martha needed new clothes. Mia picked her up and set her in the nearby crib while she finished cleaning up the changing area and brought Rosey's diaper bag over. There was no issue with the size, so she pulled out the top outfit and redressed Martha. Then she took the baby back to the infant play area and went to scrub her hands.

While the water ran, slowly warming up, Mia looked in the bathroom mirror and shuddered. Pump after pump of the soap dispenser filled her hands with a white foam that still didn't feel like enough. The water was nearly scalding now, but she let it run and run. She thought about soaping up again but knew that the director would be on her in a heartbeat if she stayed in the restroom too long. God, what a horrible job. She had to find something new.

"Boy, when they're both in the same color, they really do look alike, don't they?" The other assistant asked as Mia settled back on the floor across the blanket from the two babies in purple.

"They sure do," Mia answered but, in her head, she was wondering whether this would make her move easier or harder in the long run.

Later in the morning, as Mia watched the minute hand on the large wall clock slowly crawl toward eleven fifteen, she stole a quick look at her phone just as Julius's message arrived. *Out back, as planned. Love you, good luck!* Mia smiled to herself, pleased that she could do this for him. Once his wife was happy, Mia was convinced that she and Julius would find their own happiness, especially with a place of their own to share. She straightened her shoulders and watched as the director moved to the alarm by her desk and activated it. The harsh buzzing filled the rooms, and the babies who'd been sleeping immediately began howling, with many of the toddlers joining in. Mia watched as the teachers and other assistants scrambled around in a panic, yelling orders back and forth, the director calling out even louder to be heard over the din. Mia suddenly felt calmer than she had all day as she moved quickly to the twins' crib. She snatched the bed sheet off and bundled it around the first baby, tucking a pacifier into her mouth before covering her with the sheet. Then she picked up the other twin and walked to the hallway, where she handed her to another assistant. The toddlers and staff were all in a ragged line rushing toward the front door as Mrs. Bianchi held it open wide. Mia mimed dropping off the messy bedding and ducked left toward the laundry area. She ran, setting the bundle of baby and fabric on the top of the wide laundry cart before propping open the exit door. Then she turned and ran again until in seconds she was at the tail end of the line, then out the front door and standing around with everyone else.

13

Sandy wiped her mouth with the paper napkin and resettled it across her lap before looking over at Oscar again. It wasn't a fancy restaurant, and they were a bit ahead of the regular lunch crowd, but it didn't matter. Not at all. It was the first date they'd been on since May, and she was loving it. "I probably shouldn't have had the wine, you know."

"Why?" Oscar asked. "One glass of wine in over three months of breastfeeding is not going to make a bit of difference, and you know it." He grinned over the table at her and raised his glass in salute. "Here's to us for surviving a third of a year with twins!"

They clinked glasses and laughed, then resumed their meal. "This is so nice, Oscar. You have no idea." Before they could finish, though, both of their cell phones began to vibrate. They looked at each other and stood up quickly.

"Go," Oscar pushed Sandy toward the car. "Call and tell them we're on our way." He caught their waitress's eye and mouthed 'sorry' before throwing a wad of cash on the table and hurrying out after his wife.

The drive to the daycare center didn't take very long. Oscar glanced at the police car parked near the door and pulled his SUV up behind it, alongside the curb. He took Sandy's hand as they hurried in. There was a strange sort of buzz moving through the center, and they looked at each other before hurrying ahead to the baby room. When they got there, a tall, African American man was standing in the room with the director and two of the assistants arranged around him. Mia, the one that Oscar knew best, hurried forward. "Oh, thank God you're here. We've been calling both of your cells."

"What's going on?" Oscar spoke first as he and Sandy looked from one face to another until the director moved toward them. But Sandy wasn't waiting for anyone as she hurried toward the crib near the window that both babies usually slept in. Oscar looked over and thought that it seemed enormous with just one small infant lying in the middle of it. Sandy picked her up and held her close as she scanned the room around her. "Where's my other baby?" she demanded. "What's happened?" She came and stood beside her husband.

The man stepped forward then, and Oscar noted that a badge was clipped onto the pocket of his jeans. His right hand reached forward while a small notebook rested in his left. "I take it you're Mr. and Mrs. Wilder-Jones. I'm Officer Demetrius Smith. There's been an incident here this morning."

The director stepped up beside him. Her agitation was apparent as she fiddled with the jacket she wore, her hands reaching in and out of the pockets repeatedly. "There was a fire . . ."

"What?" Oscar shouted, and two babies in another room began to cry.

"A drill, a fire drill," the officer quickly added. "Daycares are required to hold them. My understanding is that it was a bit chaotic." He tilted his head toward the director, signaling her to continue the explanation.

"Everything went fine. We were all out front. Everyone did exactly as they were supposed to, following the rules . . ."

This time Sandy interrupted, her voice edging toward hysteria. "Where is Rosey?"

Oscar looked at the purple-clad infant she was clutching to her chest. "Isn't that Rosey?"

Sandy shook her head, and Oscar thought he heard a quick gasp behind him, but it became just a cough. "This is Martha."

"So, why's she wearing Rosey's clothes?" Oscar demanded, and Mia picked up the green diaper bag from the table. She held it open, her hands shaking slightly so that everyone could see the sunscreen smeared throughout.

"I'm sorry. When I changed her last, I couldn't use any of the clothes in here, so I borrowed one of Rosey's outfits.

"I don't care what they're wearing," Sandy's voice rose again. "I want to know where my baby is!"

An uncharacteristic silence filled the room. Oscar looked at the faces arranged around him, catching on Sandy's wet with tears. It was the officer who spoke first. "It's my understanding that once everyone was settled back inside after the drill, no one could find the second twin."

Oscar began moving around the room frantically, tossing pillows and bedding. He was racing toward the cubbies when the officer grabbed him by the arm. "Sir, we've been searching the entire church for half an hour. The baby's not here." A siren sounded in the distance, and Oscar stopped. "I've got a team coming. We're going to keep searching, but we're going to do it right." The officer asserted. "Mrs. Bianchi, you said we could use the reverend's study, is that correct?"

The siren grew closer and then cut off as it pulled into the large parking lot in front of the church. Through the window, Oscar could see other police officers emerging. With a bitter taste in his mouth, he reluctantly followed Sandy and baby Martha to meet them.

A piercing shriek, unlike anything Julius had ever heard before, filled the inside of his car. The pickup had gone so smoothly he'd been smiling to himself as he pulled away, but now? A bright red face pinched and straining, the mouth gaping wide with its shrieking, could be seen emerging from the bundle of fabric piled on the floor of the passenger seat. It was tempting to tear through the traffic and streetlights to his house, where he knew Hannah would take it from him, but he had to be careful. Nothing could draw attention to him now. He was still too close.

As the crying reached a crescendo, paused, and then began to build again, he turned up the radio and wove his way patiently through neighborhood after neighborhood, in and out of store parking lots. At last, he felt that he could safely pull up onto the highway and make his way home. Surprisingly, the steady purring of the engine on the straightaway seemed to soothe the child, and the crying finally stopped. He could still see the small face, but it was just pink now, and the eyelids were fluttering closed. He was back to feeling the triumph.

As he drove the last few miles, Julius imagined the scene at the daycare once the abduction was discovered. The night before, he'd taken some spray paint to the cameras around the perimeter of the church, so he enjoyed thinking about their frustration in reviewing the video feed. But when had churches gotten so security conscious, he wondered? When he was growing up, churches were always open and welcoming places. Then, he remembered the synagogue shooting less than a year ago, and he understood. Oh well, he put it out of his mind and shifted his thinking instead to Mia. He had grown more and more fond of her as they'd worked through their preparations, but he knew that his feelings didn't come close to matching hers. After all, he was doing this for his wife, for Hannah. He was much more interested in seeing things improve at home than he was in building a stronger relationship with Mia. But damn, he grinned, thinking. She sure had done well. He knew she had some real acting skills, too. He'd seen it as they practiced their entire routine, what came after the grab as well as before. He just said a small prayer that she was sticking with the plan and handling the aftermath.

Julius got off at his exit and pulled into the parking lot of a gas station near his home. He left the car running and held his breath as he opened the door, but the baby remained sleeping. Around back, he opened the trunk lid with the same care and extracted the infant carrier and a light blanket. He didn't bother with the seat's base since they were so close to the house. Back inside, he settled the infant seat beside him and then peeled the rumpled sheet away from the sleeping baby. He picked her up carefully, surprised again at how little she weighed, and placed her carefully in the seat. He had no idea how to do the various straps, so he just tucked the blanket around her and then headed for home. At the end of his street, he paused and texted his wife. *I have a surprise for you!*

When he pulled into the driveway, he could see Hannah standing near the front door. As she stepped outside, he saw the eager look on her face, and once again, he was that young man, in love for the first time in his life. When he emerged, the carrier in his arm and a wide grin spreading across his face, she ran into his arms, and together, they carried the small form inside.

Late on Thursday afternoon, Audrey was working at her computer when she received a text from the attorney, Gabriel. "*Jury chosen, trial set to start next Wednesday.*" A sense of dread rushed over her at the thought of facing Adams in court, but before she could text a reply, her phone flashed with a call from Sandy. It was a surprise to answer, though, and hear Oscar's voice instead.

"Audrey, I need a favor."

Audrey had never heard that tone in Oscar's voice before, and she stood up in alarm. "Anything, Oscar, what's wrong? What can I do?" She thought she heard sobbing in the background. "Is Sandy all right?"

"It's not Sandy. It's Rosey. She's gone, Audrey." His voice caught on a sob as well.

"Oh my God, was she sick? What happened?"

"No, no, it's not like that. Someone took her from the daycare center today. We're going crazy here."

There was an immediate sense of relief at knowing the baby hadn't died, but it didn't last. "What can I do, Oscar? Do you need me to come out there and help?"

"No, we're okay here. We just wanted to know if your connection to the police could help, if you could find out more than we can? They hardly told us anything."

Audrey sat back down abruptly. "What did they tell you?"

"Nothing really, they just asked us questions, over and over again. We were wrecked by the time we got back here. The officer just told us to call *them* if anyone contacted us."

"Oh my God, like a ransom request?"

"I've got no Goddamned idea." Suddenly the sound of a helicopter filled the phone, and Audrey had to hit the mute button as it reverberated through her hearing aids. When she turned the sound back on, Oscar was still talking. ". . . fucking reporters are starting to gather outside like crows."

"I'm so sorry, Oscar. I can't promise that I'll be able to learn anything useful but let me call Rod and see if there's any news."

"Thanks, Audrey." He clicked off, and Audrey sat for a moment picturing the tiny baby she'd gotten to know when she herself was recovering. She sent a quick text to her mother explaining the situation and asking her if she could go over to the house and check on them. Then, she called Rod.

"Hey Audrey, I didn't expect to hear from you today. You're not canceling on dinner tomorrow, are you?"

"Rod, Sandy's baby Rosey was taken from the daycare center today."

"Oh no! I heard the report, but they kept the name of the family out of it. I had no idea it was your friend."

"Listen, they're terrified and stumbling around in the dark trying to figure out what they should do. Oscar said the police asked them a ton of questions but didn't tell them much of anything. He wanted to know if you could find out what's going on."

There was no hesitation on his part, and Audrey thought she could hear him moving as he spoke. "Give me a little time to see what I can find out, and I'll call you back." He clicked off without a good-bye, but she knew it was because he was already focused on the request. She sat back down at her computer but had no idea how to even begin to work again. The text from Gabriel had been expected, but that didn't keep it from being frightening all the same. And now, Rosey missing on top of that? It was too much.

Audrey flipped to the local news site on her computer and saw the headlines about the kidnapping blaring already, along with a mindless video of a church parking lot and a still photo of Sandy's house. She flicked her finger to scroll past the familiar image only to land on a mug shot of Gary Adams and a brief article indicating the trial was about to begin. She was thankful that it didn't include a photograph of herself, but she could feel the reality of it all crashing down. She looked over at her front door and saw that she'd neglected to lock the deadbolt when she'd come home from the market that morning. She stood up in a panic, ran over to throw the latch, and then leaned against the front door, her heart thumping inside her chest. Sweat formed along her hairline, and she slid to the floor, bringing her head between her knees. She began tucking her hands beneath her to try and stop them from shaking. Suddenly, she could see Adams looming over her before shoving her aside. She felt the gun against her back, smelled his hot breath against her face.

"One hippopotamus, two hippopotamus, three hippopotamus." She forced herself to count, to push the air out into words even as she struggled to catch her breath. She hit the number fifty before she finally felt calm enough to stand. Once she could trust herself to walk, she pulled the business card that Gabriel had given her out of her purse and dialed the number.

"Victims' services, how may I help you?" Audrey swallowed a sob and found her voice.

Rod was moving away from his desk and down the hallway toward Smitty's as soon as Audrey finished telling him what had happened. He found the shared office area filled with activity but didn't see Smitty in the mix. He spoke with one of the uniforms that he knew. "Do you know where Smitty is? My friend's baby . . ."

"You know them? We're going crazy here. I think Smitty's over in the captain's office."

"Thanks, man." Rod smacked his shoulder and then moved on down the hall. The captain's door was open, and he could see Smitty and two uniforms standing in front of the battered, steel desk. He walked in behind them and waited for a moment while the captain was on the phone. Rod put his hand on his partner's back and leaned in. "Did you catch the baby case? It's Audrey's friend Sandy's."

Smitty's head whipped around, and he focused his eyes on Rod. "You're serious? You know these people?"

Rod nodded. "Audrey and I stopped by their place last weekend. They're panicked, and they called her, trying to see if she could get them any more information. What's going on?"

"We don't know yet. We questioned the daycare staff for a long time but didn't get anywhere." He gestured toward the captain, who was shaking his head no. "Captain's talking to the church about their video surveillance cameras from the parking lot."

The telephone call clicked off, and the captain addressed the room. "They're going to send us all of their feeds' recordings, but you were right about the cameras around back, hit with black paint." He jerked his head toward Rod. "What's he doing here?"

Rod spoke up. "Captain, they're friends of mine, the parents, the baby."

"Ah, Christ, I'm sorry." The captain rubbed his hand back and forth over his bald head and then looked up again. "So, what do you know? They got money? Should we be expecting a ransom note?"

"Money, no, not that I know of, not any more than anyone else. I think they're just ordinary people. The dad works for the electric company. Audrey's known the mom since they were kids."

Smitty spoke then. "So, if it's not for money, why was she taken?" He asked the question to the entire room, but no one seemed to have any answers.

Finally, the captain responded. He gestured toward the uniforms. "Listen, I want you two to grab a few more and get back out in that neighborhood near the daycare center. Look for any cameras you can find, shops, parking lots, traffic cameras. Hell, look for doorbell cameras." Then he turned back to Rod and Smitty. "You got anything going on right now, Rodriguez?"

"No sir, not at this moment."

"Okay, you and Smitty get out to their house, talk to the parents again. Find out what you can about them. There's got to be something we can use."

"This is my fault," Smitty commented as they headed out to the car.

Rod's head swung around. "What the hell are you talking about?"

"Shit, man, they've had me looking through cold case files for days, thought my head was going to explode. I was wishing I'd catch a fresh case, actually get to do some work again. And now this?" He raised his hand, the palm out, but Rod slapped it away before he could say any more.

"Cut the shit here. You didn't cause this, and you know it. What happened is this family got not one but two detectives to help find their baby, so get over yourself, already."

As Smitty drove, Rod sent Audrey a quick text and got Sandy's street address in return. He promised her he'd let her know the minute they learned anything new. When they pulled up, they were frustrated to find the quiet street overrun with press vans and their detritus. Smitty called in to have dispatch send some uniformed officers over to deal with the crowd. For now, Rod directed him around the block, and they pulled up in back of the house behind a delivery van. They made their way to the back door and were let in quickly. "Oh, thank God." Sandy blew out a breath and ran into Rod's arms. He held her for a moment, and then the group moved back to the living room.

"Have you found her?" Oscar asked, looking back and forth at the two detectives.

Rod spoke, hoping to reduce the level of panic in the room. "Everyone sit, please." He nodded at Audrey's mom, who'd come out of the kitchen bearing a tray with cups and saucers and a tall carafe of coffee. She set the tray on the table near the couch and began pouring everyone a cup. Rod wasn't sure whether anyone would drink it, but it did shift the focus long enough for everyone to find a seat and take a breath.

Smitty began, his voice taking on a calm, even tenor. "When we met earlier, I didn't know that you all know my partner here." He rested his hand on Rod's shoulder. "For now, he's going to help us out. I realize this is a terrifying situation so let me tell you what we've done so far and what we're planning to do next." A cry issued from somewhere upstairs, and Audrey's mother stood up quickly.

"I've got her. Don't worry." Sandy's mother mouthed, "thank you, Brigette," and then everyone's focus returned to Smitty. He took them through the steps they'd taken already, the interviews with the daycare staff, and the number of officers out scouring the area for camera images. "So, while they're doing that, we wanted to talk with you all again. What can you tell us about the daycare center? How long have your children been attending? Your routines?"

Oscar began. "The babies haven't been going there very long, just a few weeks. I usually drop them off on Tuesday and Thursday mornings on my way to work, around 7:45 or so." He gestured toward Sandy, who was watching the stairs. "Sandy picks them up at noon."

"But you were both there today for the pickup, is that right?"

Audrey's mother stepped carefully down the stairs, the cries now just a whimper. She handed the baby to Sandy and helped her spread a light blanket out so that the baby could nurse without distraction. Sandy looked over at Rod, her eyes moist with tears.

"We were having a sort of mini date. Oscar didn't have to be at work until later in the day, so we had lunch together at a restaurant."

"This wasn't a regular part of your routine?"

"No." Oscar looked at his wife and then back at Smitty. "It's the first time since the girls were born that we took a bit of time to ourselves."

"This may sound rude, and I apologize for that, but do you two think this is about money? Would you be able to pay someone to get her back? Would anyone know this?"

When the baby made a slight sound, Sandy placed her against her shoulder and began patting her on the back. "We'll pay. If someone asks, we'll pay, whatever it takes. But we'd have to borrow the money to do it." She looked at her mother, who nodded in agreement. "We'd sell the house if we had to in order to get her back, but no. We don't have the kind of money that someone would be looking for ."

Rod looked from Oscar to Sandy before speaking. "What can you tell us about the center, the people there, the setup?"

"It was my idea to take the girls there," Oscar said, dropping his head for a moment. But Sandy placed a hand on his knee, and he looked up and continued. "It's the church we go to, uh, when we go, which with twins . . ." He shrugged a shoulder, and Rod tilted his chin in encouragement. "I stopped in after work one afternoon and found out that they had space two mornings a week. Sandy didn't want to do it at first, but we needed it. We were all exhausted. We needed the help."

"And what did you think of the center once they started?" Smitty asked.

"We liked it." Sandy and Oscar answered at the same time. Then, Sandy continued. "You saw it this morning. It's small and clean and totally focused on the kids. They don't just leave the babies in their carriers or cribs; they hold them and play with them. I thought they were great."

"Did anyone on the staff stand out to you?"

"Mia, one of the assistants, was the one I spoke to the most. She usually met me at the door and helped me get the girls inside," Oscar offered.

Sandy interrupted the train of questions with renewed sobbing. "Rosey needs us! She has colic. It's hard to get her to eat sometimes." In response, baby Martha began crying, too, and the detectives stood as Sandy got up and walked Martha over near the window.

Smitty addressed the group as a whole. "All right, this is good information. Thank you. I've called for some uniforms to help with the press out there, so we're going to go and get back to work. Call us if you hear anything, and we'll be back in touch with you as quickly as we can."

Rod gave Audrey's mother a quick nod, and she acknowledged it with a wink before sitting down next to Sandy's mother and taking her hand.

The two men breathed a sigh of relief when they managed to reach their car without alerting any of the media. "I was wrong, Smitty. You're the one doing the important work. My clients are all dead."

"Amen, brother. Let's hope that's not true in this case."

Julius's delight in the entire scheme lasted a full three hours and twenty-three minutes, at which point he made an excuse to his wife and took off for the bar where he'd first met Mia. He ordered a double before his butt even touched the stool and hung his head in his hands as he waited.

The first hour and a half had been utter bliss. His wife Hannah had totally bought his lame story about the adoption agency having contacted him at work. She didn't seem alarmed by the lack of supplies or preparations for the child. After all, she'd been stocking an entire nursery for a year just in case. She cooed and smiled at the infant and held the child to her chest, swaying gently as she sent Julius back and forth, setting everything into place. Soon, she had the baby changed and was checking her supply of formula to see that it was still good. She directed him through the proper preparation of the bottle and then settled into her rocking chair to nurse her first child. Julius couldn't remember the last time he'd seen her that happy.

The baby hadn't cared for the bottle, though, and a rapid, piercing, shrieking sound began and continued unabated until he made his hasty departure. He was fizzing with rage as he sucked down the first drink and ordered another. It didn't help that the television above the bar was filled with news and images centered on the baby's abduction. In a fury, he did the one thing he'd forbidden Mia from doing. He pulled out the small burner phone they'd been using and texted her.

She was there in less than ten minutes, and he followed her through the kitchen and around to the back of the building. A set of scraggly trees screened the streetlight from a worn-out old picnic table that had been hacked and painted and left to rot. Neither of them noticed.

"What the flaming fuck is wrong with that kid? It won't quit screaming!" He hissed at Mia as she leaned one knee on the bench.

"I'm sorry, Julius, it's the wrong twin. I meant to grab the healthy one, the nice one, but their clothes got . . ."

He interrupted her. "You grabbed a sick kid. Are you shitting me?" Before he even thought about what he was doing, he shoved her hard, knocking her to the ground. She fell awkwardly, her head hitting the ground before the rest of her body with a sound that he knew immediately wasn't good. He watched in horror as blood began pooling behind her head and onto the concrete slab beneath the table. He squatted down next to her, touching her face, calling to her. "Mia, Mia, I'm so sorry. Mia, talk to me. Come on, honey, wake up." Her eyes were open as if she were about to say something, but they stayed that way, unblinking, and he could tell it was no use. He rested his ear against her chest but heard nothing. God above, what would he do now? He couldn't stand seeing her like that, utterly still with those lovely blue eyes staring vacantly at him, so he pulled off his jacket and laid it over her face. He stepped back away from the little copse of trees and studied the dark alley around him. He had to get her out of there.

He walked quickly, clinging to the side of the next building as he made his way in the darkness, dashing ahead to where his car was parked. It was an old, navy blue Buick whose few bits of chrome had fallen off years ago. Without turning on the lights, he started the car and then pulled out into the street, passing a line of parked cars before reaching the corner. He waited until the street was empty of vehicles before turning the corner and then pulling on down the narrow alley. He paused, then slowly backed the car up next to the table and opened his trunk. He pulled out the car seat base and tossed it onto the floor of the back seat. Then he gathered up Mia, pulled his jacket tightly around her face, and folded her into the trunk. It was pitch dark, but he could sense that blood was dripping everywhere. He stood frozen for a moment, unsure of what he should do. Finally, he heard another car starting down the mouth of the alley, so he slammed the trunk shut, jumped behind the wheel, and drove away from the site. Blood smeared along the steering wheel, but he wiped it off with his sleeve.

He drove aimlessly at first, turning away from cars as they approached, circling one block after another until he found himself alongside a concrete wall covered with old graffiti. A light shown ahead of him, and he spotted a carwash with a 24-hour banner flashing repeatedly against the black night. He turned his lights off and pulled quietly into an unlighted bay on the far end. He rolled down his window and sat listening to the sounds around him. There was no attendant in sight, but his heart nearly stopped when he heard a siren begin to wail. It grew fainter as he waited, though, until everything was quiet again. He was relieved that there didn't seem to be a whole lot going on in the area. A church across the street was massive but dark. Whatever it offered had clearly finished for the night.

He pulled out his regular phone, dimming the bright display screen before using an app to see what was around him. His thumb flicked around the small screen until he spotted an edge of blue just down the street from where he was hiding. He pulled up a street view of the area and discovered what looked like an old warehouse with a riverside dock in the back. It appeared dark enough in the photo, so he dropped the phone on the seat next to him and eased the car out of the washing bay and back onto the street. With his lights still off, he made his way down the road until he saw the warehouse building looming ahead. There was a chain with a lock dangling from a post at the entrance, but once he was closer, he could see that it was rusted and hanging useless. He continued on around the back of the building until he could see the dock, the dark river swirling around its base.

He pulled up as close as he could get and was relieved to find that the building cast a deep shadow over the entire area. He flicked off the dome light before stepping outside of the car and then paused, waiting, counting out several minutes as he listened to the area around him. But there was nothing that he could detect, no cars, no people, nothing. He went to the trunk and opened it, the small light there just enough for him to see the body. Bile rose in his throat, and he waited, clenching his hands until the nails dug into the flesh of his palms, and he could master his breathing once again. He held his breath as he searched her, reaching into every pocket, fishing out her two phones and a few credit cards that were sandwiched between several bills. Seven dollars, that was all she'd had on her, he thought, the guilt washing over him in a thick wave. He hung his head for a moment, pictured her lovely face and body again, tears filling his eyes. Just then, a gust of wind disturbed a nearby bird, its bright shriek filling the air with a chilling cry. His heart quickened, and he resumed his search, making sure that there was nothing identifying left on the body at all. He walked the perimeter then, checking all around him before chucking the phones far out into the river. Then he returned to the trunk and lifted her body out.

At the edge of the dock, he could sense the movement of the water, the current that he hoped would carry her body far away from where he stood. He knelt, pulling his jacket away from her face briefly, not sure what he should say in the way of good-bye, but it was too dark to see. Her face was lost in the night's shadows, so he pulled the jacket back up and tucked it around her. Reaching behind her, he found the catch and zipped it up as far as he could, pinning her arms against her. Then he rolled her body carefully toward the edge and dropped her into the water. The jacket ballooned with air for a long moment before the water seemed to suck the whole body down and away.

Unsure what to do next, Julius figured his priority was to get rid of the car. He drove back to the car wash and pulled again into the un-lighted bay. Although the light was out, the water and scrub brush were still functioning. He dug the required coins out of the well in the car's console and dropped them into the machine. He started at the noise it made and managed to splash himself with the reflected spray before fumbling with the mechanism and finally directing the hose. He knew there was no way he could eliminate all the evidence. He just wanted to clean the outside enough that it wouldn't be obvious once he'd abandoned the car. He remembered a run-down, old, secondhand car lot north of the city that didn't seem to be thriving. He decided he'd try and dump the car there, where hopefully it would go unnoticed for some time. Once he'd rinsed the car off the best he could, he pulled off his wet work shirt and threw it in the back seat. The t-shirt underneath was wet as well, but it didn't seem to have as much blood on it. He pulled out of the lot, checking his surroundings carefully again, before heading up the street, away from the river. He drove more than six blocks before daring to turn the headlights on.

He headed north, deliberately taking a few of the busier streets, mixing into the late-night activity. The downtown area was still busy and well-lit, with folks out and about in the warm night air. He did his best to blend with the traffic flow until he was beyond the busiest areas. Then he sped up, taking a circuitous route before pulling into the car lot. There were plenty of lights and signs, but the end of the last two rows of cars were both deep in shadow. He pulled in beside another, nearly identical old Buick and killed his lights. Using the flashlight on his phone, he searched his car's interior, filling a discarded plastic bag with his shirt and Mia's things as well as all the junk that the vehicle's front seat and glove box had accumulated. He stepped out and rested the bag on the car's trunk, then took out a penknife and removed the license plate, attaching it to the car next to him.

The other Buick was locked, and he was prepared to break a window, but he tried his key anyway, shocked when it opened the door. He'd read about the possibility but was surprised to find that it actually worked. His key didn't work in the ignition, though, so he searched under the seat before flipping down the visor, hoping that the car's keys might be left accessible. Sure enough, they dropped into his lap. He looked around him at the deserted lot. It was nearly two in the morning. Suddenly a deer caught his eye, wandering along the line of trees at the back edge of the lot. It seemed unhurried, and Julius took that as a good sign. He started the car and pulled the second Buick out of line, then got out and moved his car into its place. He returned to the new vehicle and dropped his own keys into the well of the console.

He had to get home. He got onto the highway and drove past his exit, taking the next one and circling until he spotted an abandoned gas station. He pulled up beside a gaping dumpster in the back and emptied the bag of items from his car, doing his best to scatter them among the garbage before dropping the keys in with them. Then, he drove home as quickly and carefully as he could. He didn't think he'd taken a full breath until he pulled into his driveway. When he walked in, his wife Hannah was dozing in the rocking chair, the infant sleeping peacefully in her arms. He made his way upstairs quietly and stepped into the bathroom. With the light on, he was shocked at the amount of blood on him. He pulled off his clothes, piling them together in one corner of the bathroom floor. Then, he took a blazing hot shower. Afterwards, he pulled on his robe and carefully folded the clothes into a ball, the bloodied parts on the inside. In the bedroom, he tucked the ball of clothes into his briefcase and snapped it shut. He would need to dispose of them on his way to work in the morning. Finally, he collapsed back onto the bed and stared at the ceiling, numb with fear and shock. Thank God Hannah had been sleeping when he walked in.

18

By the time Rod and Smitty were ready to leave the missing infant's home, a pair of black and whites had arrived and were dealing with the press. Rod took over the driving and nodded his thanks to one of the officers he knew before heading back downtown.

"Vultures," Smitty offered, but Rod shook his head.

"Nah, they're a pain in the ass, I know, but they're just stiffs trying to do their jobs the same as us. It's not their fault that the news has devolved into what it is these days."

Smitty looked at his partner. "Devolved, huh? You been spending time with your thesaurus while I was laid up? Devolved. What kind of word is that?"

"What's the matter, don't you know what it means?"

"Of course I do, asshole. I just didn't think you did." Smitty laughed but clutched at his stomach when Rod threatened to punch him for his remarks. "Hey man, you crazy?"

"Geez, you get to say whatever shit you like, and I have to take it. Is that where we are?"

"You got it, my brother. That is the current lay of the land."

"Well, shit." Rod drove in silence then, the afternoon drawing to a close, the light beginning to fade earlier than he liked. He always hated the end of summer, the days drawing shorter and shorter until winter would have them all once again. He looked over at his partner. "So, where should we start?"

Smitty had a tablet open in front of him and was reviewing the information they'd taken down already. "I think we need to go back at the daycare staff, maybe bring them into the station where they won't be quite so comfortable."

"Tonight, you mean?"

"No, I don't think we'll get any more from them tonight. Let's let them sweat it out a bit. I think we should take a look at the video."

"The captain had them collecting everything they could find. It'll take a while."

"I'm sure. Let's pick up some food on our way in." He pulled out his phone and began punching in their order as Rod wove his way through the early evening traffic.

The precinct quieted as they settled into desks in the missing persons area, take-out containers in their laps, both computers up and ready to scroll through different video feeds. Rod pointed his plastic fork toward Smitty's computer. "Okay. Let's look at the church's video first." The two of them watched the feed from the various cameras upfront before switching to the ones in the back. "How far back can we go on these, do you know?"

Smitty pulled out his tablet again, shaking his head. "The pastor said the cameras were on a 7-day loop that reset every Wednesday at midnight."

"Why Wednesdays?"

"I don't know. Their main services are Sunday morning and Wednesday evening, so that's just how they set it up."

"Well, let's back it up as far as we can." They watched as the video ran in a black, uninterrupted blur until a few frames lit up the screen. "There, there's a bit." Rod looked at the time stamp that ran beneath the images. From that camera, there was nothing to be seen but the pavement in front of the backdoor. But Rod and Smitty pulled up the other feeds, quickly backing all of them up to the few minutes after midnight that were visible.

Smitty paused the one on his unit. "Look at the time. You can see the order that they were painted in." The backdoor camera had been the first to go, then two forward from it and two around by a side door. Finally, the camera at the farthest exit went black. Each camera had caught just a flicker of a vehicle, and the two men struggled to pair up the images. "What are you seeing?"

"It's tough, man, a sedan of some kind, big, dark, not very new. I can't see a plate, though, can you?"

They both ran the videos forward and back, each time trying to pinpoint what they were seeing. "This is like that old poem about six blind men describing an elephant. The pieces just don't add up to anything coherent." Rod tossed his empty container on the desk beside him.

"Let's move our perimeter out and look at the traffic cams in the area. You go east. I'll go west."

With the time frame in mind, the task became marginally less tedious, but it was still after midnight before they had reached any sort of tentative conclusion. Smitty stood and gathered the food containers, sweeping the entire mess into a bin near the door. "We need to get some sleep, or we're going to be worthless tomorrow. Let's meet back here at 7:30, and we'll take what we've got into the captain."

"It's not much, a hunch on the model, one number on a plate?" Smitty shut off the monitors, and the two of them began moving toward the door.

"Hey, it's a good start. We'll get some techs in here in the morning and see what they can make out of it."

Rod clapped a gentle hand on Smitty's back. He could see the fatigue hitting his friend, and it made him angry once again at the shooters. "Get some sleep, buddy, okay?"

Smitty gave him a half-hearted salute, and they headed to their separate cars. Rod couldn't help thinking back to the weekend visit he and Audrey had made. He waited until he saw his partner safely on his way, then turned his car off and headed back inside. He figured he had another couple of hours that he could give to the search. He knew Sandy and Oscar deserved however much he could give.

"Thanks, Mom. I'm sorry I couldn't get out there, but I'm glad you could be with them." Audrey's mother had called her that evening, once she'd returned home, and was able to give Audrey a report on Sandy and her family as well as an account of the detectives' visit.

"I'm going to go back over in the morning and see what I can do to help. Cecelia is supposed to meet with the orthopedist tomorrow, and I'm afraid she'll cancel after everything that's happened."

"Oh, I hope you can talk her into keeping the appointment. She's in so much pain."

"I know, honey, I know. I'll check in with you tomorrow."

"Okay, Mom, good night." Audrey walked back and forth in front of her sofa, frustrated at being sidelined for all that was going on. She'd been at the station house earlier in the morning once she and the forensics team returned from an unattended death out on the edge of the county. But that had been before the news broke about Rosey. It was clear that the missing infant was getting *a lot* of attention from the department now, but no one seemed to have any additional information. Rod had texted Audrey earlier, letting her know that he and Smitty would be picking up take-out and looking through video all evening.

There was nothing to do but try to sit down and work. The woman she'd spoken with at victims' services had found a cancellation and made her an appointment to see a counselor early the next morning. Audrey would be on call for the police after that. Then Saturday, she had Katy's bridal shower and Sunday morning, a small wedding to photograph at the Heinz Chapel. She opened her laptop and settled into work, but rather than pulling up the last wedding she'd done, instead, she found herself drawn to the pictures she'd taken at home last weekend. She'd caught some great shots of Sandy with her babies, her mother Cecelia cheering on her baseball team, and Oscar walking in, both arms loaded with groceries. There was such joy in all of the photos, she thought. She flicked through them slowly, finally landing on one slightly crooked shot that Sandy had taken of Audrey holding Rosey. Looking at the photo, she could remember clearly how Rosey felt in her arms, the weight, the scent of her, the soft hair around Rosey's ear that tickled Audrey as she bent in for a kiss. "Rosey, love, are you safe?" Audrey forced herself to imagine the infant sleeping and whispered a small prayer that whoever had taken her wanted her kept alive.

Bright and early the next morning, Audrey was trying to decide what she thought about the counselor she'd been assigned to talk to. She was relieved that it was not a man, but she wasn't sure that the round-faced, grandmotherly-looking woman was up to the task. Audrey had spent the first ten minutes describing her ordeal as the woman sat quietly writing notes on what looked like a battered old legal pad.

"All right, now tell me what's been going on since then."

Audrey paused, wondering why it seemed easier to describe the attack than it was to describe what she'd been experiencing since then. The silence grew.

With a gentle voice, the woman began. "I'm guessing maybe some bad dreams, a sense of panic when you leave your apartment, maybe a reluctance to leave even? Do you find yourself reliving the attack?" She lifted her tone in question.

Audrey blinked but found it difficult to speak. She squeezed her hands in front of her and looked up into the older woman's face. "You're right, with all of it. It's been months, though, and I thought it was getting better, but now . . ."

"The trial is coming up, isn't that what you said?"

"Yes, Wednesday of next week."

"So that's shifted everything into high gear. You're going to have to see him, to hear and talk about the attack. The idea is overwhelming, isn't it?"

Audrey sagged back in her chair and nodded. "I used to feel so strong before this happened, put together, you know?"

"I do know, and then he swept all that confidence away, didn't he? Cuts and bruises heal, but it's a lot harder to heal your sense of self-worth."

"So, what can I do now? I don't want to look weak. I don't want to feel weak when I'm at the trial."

"Tell me about your support system. Who have you turned to so far?"

"Well, my parents, of course, and my friends. My boyfriend is a detective, so I've been leaning on him a lot. But . . ."

"Will he be able to sit with you?"

Audrey shook her head. "No, he's being called as a witness, so he can't attend."

"What about your parents and friends?"

"Have you heard about the baby that was kidnapped?"

"From the daycare center? Yes."

"It's my friend Sandy's baby. Her mom has some health issues right now, so my mom's been helping out. I know they'd all be there to support me, but if Rosey isn't found by then, I think Sandy and her mother will need my mom with them." Audrey looked up. "I guess that leaves my dad."

"Have you called and talked to him about all of this? Does he know you've been struggling?"

Audrey pulled a worn tissue from her pocket and dabbed at her eyes before continuing. "No, I haven't said too much about it to anyone. Rod, my boyfriend, I think he suspects something. I've had a few bad dreams when I was with him."

The woman leaned back in her chair and folded the pages of the legal pad back down. "Then that's where I think you should start. Call your dad. Be honest about how you've been feeling and let him know how important it will be for you to have him with you at the trial. Do you think you can do that?"

Audrey took a deep breath and let it out. "I think I can."

"All right," the counselor pulled out an old-fashioned pocket calendar. "Let's see. You said it starts on Wednesday. How about if you and your dad come and see me on Tuesday afternoon for a chat around 3:15?"

Audrey tucked the tissue away and stood. "Thank you. I'll do that. And thank you for seeing me so quickly this morning. I know I shouldn't have been putting this off."

"It's okay, honey. We all have our own path to follow in our own time."

"Were you?" Audrey paused.

The counselor nodded briefly. "Yes, I was, but that's a story for another day. I'll see you on Tuesday."

Audrey walked the few blocks to the bus stop and stood leaning against a bank building as she waited with the others. She sent her dad a quick text. "*Can I call you later?*"

By the time she boarded, he'd sent a response. "*Of course, any time.*"

Rod had fallen into bed sometime after two-thirty but was awake immediately when the alarm began buzzing at six. His first thought was of Simple Simon, how hard it often was to get the old dog up and moving at such an early hour. Then the loss hit him again, and for just a moment, he buried his face in the pillow, pulling the ends of it up around his ears. He wished that Audrey was there with him, and he wondered whether they'd be able to keep their date for dinner or not. Suddenly, the needs of the day overrode the sense of loss, and he propelled himself toward the bathroom.

Just over an hour later, he walked into the station house, a tall travel mug filled with coffee in one hand, the end of a granola bar in the other. He shoved the last bite into his mouth and dropped the wrapper on top of an overflowing can. Then, he grabbed an apple out of the basket that sat on the dispatcher's desk, gave her a quick nod of thanks, and headed down the hall to missing persons. He wasn't surprised to find Smitty already engrossed in more video feeds. Rod tapped his hand on his friend's shoulder and sat down next to him. "Anything new?"

Smitty turned, gripped his hands around the armrests of his chair, and looked hard at his partner. "You mean since you left here last night?" Smitty slammed his hand on the desk. "Man, do not fucking baby me. I hate that shit. You sent me home and then snuck back in here, admit it. You think I don't have what it takes. I'm insulted, man."

Rod was taken aback by the level of anger and hurt on his partner's face. He shook his head as he raised his hands in front of him in defense. "I swear, man, it was not like that at all. I was in my car, I was right behind you, ready to go, but then this image of Audrey holding Rosey up in the air popped into my head, and it just grabbed me." He let his head and hands drop. "It left me wanting to do a little more, that's all. I'm sorry, I know you've got this." Smitty seemed to study Rod's face for a moment before turning back to his monitor.

"Okay, I'll believe that once, just once, you hear me?"

"Got it."

"The techs are due here in a few minutes, so we're going to turn all this feed over to them. They'll take the bits we've got on the car and try to match it up with traffic cams around the area. We know what time he sprayed the cameras and what time the baby was taken, so they'll work with all of that."

"What's up for us then?"

"I've got most of the staff lined up to come in and talk with us again this morning."

Rod mimed looking at a nonexistent watch. "You woke them up?"

"Bet your ass I did. The boss is coming in first, then the teachers. They're keeping the center open today since it's a workday, so they're coming in one by one."

"What about the assistant that Oscar mentioned, Mia, the one they seemed to know a little better?"

Smitty rubbed his hands back and forth quickly. "That's the snag. I can't reach her. I've tried her cell, but it goes directly to voice mail. The owner said that she has a current address for Mia but that she'd heard she was housesitting for someone and probably wouldn't be there. Apparently, she liked to do that, get out of her place when she could."

"Well, that's not good."

"No, it isn't."

"Do you mind if I go out to the center, look around some while you're meeting with the folks here? If I see her there, I can send her your way."

"Sounds good. Hey, you think Audrey'd go with you? She's got the eye, you know, might spot something we missed?"

"I'll check." Rod nodded in agreement and pulled out his phone as he made his way back out toward the car. He was pleased when she answered so quickly but concerned when he heard her voice.

"Rod, is there any word?" He felt bad knowing that the call would have gotten her hopes up.

"I'm sorry, no, nothing yet. Listen, Smitty's going to be meeting with the staff at the precinct, so I'm heading back to the daycare center. You free to come with?"

"Yeah," he heard the hesitation in her voice. "I just finished an appointment, but no calls have come in yet."

"Are you all right? Is this a bad time?"

There was a pause, and he waited, wondering what was bothering her this morning. "I'm okay. I can tell you about my appointment when you get here."

"Okay, if you're sure. I'll pick you up in a few minutes."

She wasn't on her steps when he pulled up, so he left the car double-parked and rang the bell. In just a moment, she was at the door, but he didn't think she looked quite herself. "Are you all right? Are you sure you're up for this? I know it's got to be hard."

Audrey followed him out and climbed into the car. She fastened her belt and rested her hands in her lap. "It's not about Rosey. I went to see someone in victims' services this morning, a counselor."

"Was it helpful?" He pulled into the line of traffic as he waited for her response.

"I guess I'm not sure yet. It did help to tell someone how I've been feeling."

"I've been wondering a bit, but you haven't said much about it to me."

"I know. I've been embarrassed and mad at myself for not getting over the whole thing."

"Audrey, there's no reason to be embarrassed or mad. I still have moments when I see you in your apartment all beaten to hell. I was scared to death."

"Thank you for saying that. The thing is, in my head, I know what's real and what isn't. I know that I'm safe now, but when the panic hits, everything just flies out the window, and I'm back in it. With the trial getting ready to start, knowing I'm going to have to see him there, everything's just gotten a little more intense."

"Did the counselor have any suggestions for you? I hate like hell that I can't be in the courtroom with you."

"It's all right. It's just that now with everything going on with Sandy, they really need my mom with them. So that just leaves my dad for support. The counselor suggested I talk with him about it all. She offered to see us together on Tuesday."

"That sounds like a good idea. I like your dad. I think he'll be great."

"I should have said something to them earlier, I know. I just didn't want them to worry."

"Believe me. They've been plenty worried. They'll be glad to have you let them in on it a bit."

"Have they said something to you?"

He waggled his head from side to side. "Not exactly, but they drop the occasional hints. I think they might have heard one of your nightmares."

Audrey looked over. "You noticed them, huh? They've gotten better lately."

He reached his hand over and rested it on hers. "I noticed. It woke Simon up one night when you called out, and the poor guy was nearly deaf. I'm sorry, I should have spoken with you about them. I didn't want to intrude, you know?"

She clasped his hand in both of hers. "I don't think I've been ready to talk about it till now. I just called the center yesterday after pulling myself up out of a pity pool by my front door. They had a cancellation, or I'd have never gotten in so soon."

"A pity pool, huh? I have a tough time picturing that."

"Let's just leave it all for now, is that okay? Can I talk to you about it later when I'm feeling a little more put together?"

He squeezed her hand before taking his back and making the turn into the church parking lot. "Of course. Let's see what we can find out here, okay?"

Rod drove around the circular drive in back, showing Audrey first the side and then the back where the cameras had been painted black. Then he parked, and they headed in. "Do you know this church?"

Audrey shook her head. "No, we weren't the church-going types. I went with Sandy to a few programs here, but I don't remember much."

They followed the signs directing them to the childcare center, but it was soon apparent that very few children had come in that morning. Rod unfolded his badge and showed it to the young woman in the first room. Audrey hung her name badge around her neck, and the two of them were allowed in.

The first woman hurried off, but a young woman with short, cropped hair and dark eyes met them as they entered. "Detective, I'm Ronnell Washington, the assistant director." The three of them shook hands, and she led them on into the room. "This is our toddler room, but as you can see, only a few children came in today." Her face reflected the deep worry that he imagined all the staff were experiencing in the wake of the abduction. "I think some parents were afraid of the place, and some were afraid of the press."

"We didn't see any press when we came in." Rod offered, and the young woman shook her head.

"No, the Reverend spoke with a few of them early this morning, and then they left. It's been quiet since then." Rod noticed that Audrey seemed to tune her out as she began looking around her carefully.

"Ms. Washington, can you take us through Oscar's routine? What he did when he dropped off the babies in the morning?"

"Sure," she signaled to an older woman in the next doorway to take her place and then led them down the hallway. "Mia usually met Mr. Wilder-Jones and helped him with the girls in the morning."

"Is she here?" Rod asked. "We'd like to talk with her."

"No, I thought she was with Mrs. Bianchi at the police station."

"She's not. Do you have a number for her? Do you know where she lives?"

"No, I'm sorry. I have her cell, but Mia stayed in all different places. She mentioned having a roommate, but I don't think they got along very well, and their place was rather small. I think that's why Mia likes housesitting or pet sitting whenever she can." The young woman continued the tour, indicating the cubbies where the diaper bags were kept, the changing areas, and play space.

"What do you remember from early yesterday morning? Did anything stand out to you?"

"Not really, well, except seeing the twins in the same clothes, that was weird. Mia said something had spilled all over Martha's bag, so she had to put her in one of Rosey's outfits when she changed her. It was a little funny seeing them together like that."

"Anything else you can remember? Tell us about the fire drill."

Ronnell Washington quickly clamped her hands over her ears. "Oh my God, it was so loud. The alarm was making this horrible buzzing sound, and the babies all started crying. The toddlers, some of them were screaming too. Mrs. Bianchi kept yelling at us, telling us what door to use, where to line up. It was crazy."

"Was everyone outside then?" Rod held open the front door as Ronnell led them through, following the route the drill had taken.

"Yes, I was in front, carrying one of the baby carriers and holding a toddler by the hand. Everyone had a baby or child in their hands, I think. We were all standing around here waiting for the alarm to stop so that we could go back inside."

"Ms. Washington, can you point out where you think everyone was standing during the drill?" Rod used both hands to indicate the area around them.

"Sure, the teachers were trying to corral the toddlers, keep the ones who could walk from getting away from us." She gestured around her to the left. "The others were all holding babies, even Mrs. Bianchi. I remember seeing her hand one of them to Mia."

"Mia's hands were empty?" Audrey asked. She watched as Ronnell tipped her head to the side in puzzlement.

"I know she came rushing out the door with us, just after Mrs. Bianchi, I think. But I'm not sure she had a baby with her."

"But Mrs. Bianchi did?"

"That's right."

"And what happened after the drill?" Rod continued as they turned and went back inside.

She gestured around her as she spoke. "We all came back in the same door and took the children to the different rooms. It was time for the toddlers to eat, so I was helping one of the girls get the food ready."

"And the others? Do you know what the other staff members were doing?"

The young woman shrugged. "Not really. As I said, I was helping get the food ready. I could hear that a few of the babies were still crying, so I imagine the others were taking care of them, probably feeding some and changing others."

"And the director, Mrs. Bianchi? Do you know where she was?"

Ronnell Washington directed them to follow her toward a cluttered desk that sat in the corner. She pointed at the old-fashioned telephone sitting on the desk. "I think she was talking with someone about the drill, but I don't know who. I couldn't hear her very clearly."

"Had the drill gone well?" Audrey asked.

"I think we did okay. We were out pretty quickly, and I know we did better than last time. We nearly lost our certificate over that one, so Mrs. Bianchi had been warning us about the drill for weeks."

"Then everyone knew when it was scheduled?" Rod indicated the rooms all around them.

She reached around him to pull open the desk drawer, then picked up a day planner and flipped back a page. "We told the staff that it was coming but not when exactly. Only Mrs. Bianchi and I knew exactly what time it was planned for." She held up the page with the time of the drill clearly marked.

"Could anyone have seen this ahead of time?" Rod took the planner and began paging back through it.

"Well, it's Mrs. Bianchi's, but it's usually right here in the desk, so I guess it's possible for someone to look at it. I never saw anyone pick it up, though."

A toddler shrieked in the next room, and she excused herself to go and check on it while Rod and Audrey looked at the other items left out on the director's desk. "So, what are you thinking?" Audrey asked.

"I think this was planned for a while." He set the planner back on the desk. "Let's take a look at the rest of the church."

Together they walked down the long hallway looking into the various classrooms. Those on the opposite side from the daycare center were obviously for older children and probably were used for Sunday school classes or other community groups. One short hallway led to a small kitchen on one side and what appeared to be a laundry room on the other with an outside door at the end. Rod and Audrey walked around the kitchen first, but it was clean and well-ordered and offered no new information. Across from the kitchen, the laundry room held a front-loading washer and dryer unit against the back wall. A large rolling cart was half-filled with what looked like bed linens, and a table against the right side was stacked with sheets, towels, and washcloths.

Audrey peered into the rolling cart and lifted out a wet towel from the top. "I wonder what was in here yesterday?" she asked, and Rod made a note to check with Smitty and his search team. Stepping out of the small room, Rod reached for the outer door. It had an emergency door indicator on it, so he braced for the noise it would make, but when he pushed it open, there was no sound from the alarm. He looked up at Audrey.

"And what's the story with this, huh?" he added. They returned to the daycare area and spoke with Ronnell Washington once more. When she couldn't explain the door's alarm malfunctioning, Rod thanked her and stepped outside with Audrey.

The day was warm, but a breeze was coming up that Rod thought might bring rain. He leaned against the car and dialed his partner. "Smitty, how's it going?"

"We're hearing a lot about the fire drill. What about you?"

"Yeah, I think we need to keep on with that. The time and date for it were written in a planner that the director keeps in her desk. Anyone could have known. Also, I want to talk with someone from your search team yesterday. There's an emergency door that's not working, could have been the way out."

"You got it. Any word on Mia? Is she there working today?"

"No, and the woman we spoke to didn't know how to reach her other than the cell number we've got."

"Doesn't feel right, does it?"

"Not at all. Listen, send one or two of your guys from yesterday back out here, would you?" He saw Audrey's phone alert and watched as she stepped away to take a call. "After I'm done here, I'm going to check out the address that we've got for Mia, see if I can talk to someone about her. Maybe the roommate knows something."

Rod clicked off and then turned to see Audrey. "You get a call?"

"Yeah, I've got to go. I've got a ride coming, so you're good here."

"All right. I guess I'm not sure whether dinner is going to work out for tonight or not. I'll have to give you a call later when I can." Audrey reached up and kissed him on the cheek, and he held her against him for a moment. "Be careful, okay? Do you know where you're going?"

Audrey shook her head. "Not yet. Good luck, Rod. I hope I hear from you soon. Maybe Mia has Rosey at her place, and we can get her back to Oscar and Sandy today."

Rod kissed her and held her tight for one more moment, then released her when two cars pulled into the lot. Audrey got in the first and left while Rod waited for the policemen who were getting out of the second. He hoped to God Audrey's optimism was well-founded. He just couldn't seem to feel it himself.

21

Julius lay in bed well past the time when he should have risen for work, his arm flung over his eyes, his stomach roiling with acid and unease. Earlier, he had heard Hannah calling his supervisor and telling him he was sick. He appreciated that gesture, knew it was her way of being kind. She wanted time for them to be together, to start being a family, but he couldn't seem to make himself get up. Three or four times during the night, the baby had awakened, crying. Each time Hannah had patted him gently on the leg and gotten up to see to the child. Now the baby was screaming again, and he wondered just how long Hannah's patience would last.

Once he'd splashed water on his face and pulled on clean sweatpants and a T-shirt, he made his way to the kitchen. His wife was standing with her back to the window, the screaming child resting on her shoulder, Hannah's hand ceaselessly patting the infant as she sang a quiet song. "Good morning," Hannah called to him, her voice cheerful even over the din.

Julius saluted her with his coffee cup before setting it down and peeling a banana. "How are you doing this morning? You didn't get much sleep last night, did you?"

"Oh," she waved her hand dismissively, "new mothers never get much sleep. It comes with the territory."

"But why does she cry so much?"

"I've done a lot of reading on this, and I think it's colic. There doesn't seem to be any kind of pattern for when she cries, and even when she stops, she's still fussy."

"Does she need a doctor?" Julius swallowed hard, struggling to imagine how they would ever manage a doctor visit with the level of alarm about the abduction still palpable in the city.

But Hannah's manner seemed unconcerned. "No, we can take care of her. We'll just hold her and cuddle her as long as she needs. Babies outgrow colic. It's just a matter of time. Would you like to hold her?"

The baby had quieted some, but there was a stiffness to her even as Hannah tried to put her into Julius's arms. He couldn't help but recoil from it.

"Oh, don't be nervous, honey. She's our baby, now. She'll be wanting her daddy, you'll see."

Julius stood, picked up his coffee cup. He edged away from the child and leaned against the counter, trying his best to steady his raw nerves. "Have you thought of a name for her yet?"

Hannah's smile seemed to be lit from within, and Julius was suddenly overwhelmed by the happiness he saw on her face. "I thought maybe we'd call her Joy since that's what she's brought us. What do you think?"

Julius thought that the red, pinch-faced infant was probably the least joyful creature he'd seen in a long time, but he smiled anyway, kissed his wife on the cheek, and moved toward the backdoor. "I think that sounds perfect."

The morning sun was warming the back porch, and he stood in its heat, willing the light to fill him up, to cleanse him of the night's disaster. A butterfly settled on the back of the plastic chair, and Julius watched as it gently opened and shut its wings, staring at him the whole time. Mia, he thought, I'm so sorry, so very, very sorry. When he could stand it no longer, he waved his hand in a wide arc until the butterfly took flight. Then, he collapsed onto the worn chair and dropped his head, scrubbing his hands over the rough whiskers, wondering what in the world he should do next.

In the morning, Audrey's mother Brigitte used the spare key to let herself into the Wilder-Jones house by way of the kitchen door. She knew it always used to be unlocked, once welcoming Audrey and Sandy's other friends while Brigitte and a few other mothers were stuck at work. Sandy's house, filled with siblings and pets and all of the wonderful confusion that came with it, had been a key part of Audrey's childhood. Cecelia had always been there for her when Brigitte had had to work, and she was determined that she would be here for her friend now. "Good morning," she called as she closed the screen door quietly behind her.

The kitchen was a mess, with cups and paper plates scattered everywhere. Brigitte started a fresh pot of coffee before getting to work clearing everything away. Halfway through, Cecelia came in, walking slowly, clutching the back of each chair before pulling one out and carefully lowering herself into it. "Oh Brigitte, you didn't have to do that."

"Hush, Cecelia, now just hush." Brigitte brought a fresh mug of coffee and set it down on the table, squeezing her friend's shoulder. "What would you like to eat? I think I saw some milk in the refrigerator and some eggs. Can I fix you something?"

Cecelia pointed to a loaf of bread that had nearly been squashed by a takeout container. "I hate to trouble you, but maybe, just a piece of toast? Do you mind? I know this coffee will eat right through me if I don't have a little something."

Brigitte filled the four slots with bread and then brought out butter and a jar of jam while it toasted. "Is this some of yours?" Brigitte turned the glass jam-jar toward her friend and unscrewed the silver ring. She was pleased to see a smile cross her friend's face, if only for a second.

"Yes, that's the last of the strawberry from this summer. I was hoping to get some apple butter started soon, but . . ." Her voice drifted off as Brigitte brought the toast and coffee carafe over to the table. Once everything was ready, she sat down beside her friend.

"What time is your appointment this morning?"

"Oh, I couldn't go out now. What if the police call? I need to be here for Sandy."

Brigitte stretched her hand out and rested it on Cecelia's. "You're in pain, Cecelia."

"Oh, that's nothing new."

Brigitte interrupted her with a voice that had a sterner edge to it than she normally used. "Pain itself, living with that kind of pain, Cecelia, is its own kind of disease. How are you going to be there for your family if you won't take care of yourself?"

"But today, not today. I couldn't think of going today."

"You can and you will," a deep voice spoke as Oscar entered the kitchen, a sleeping Martha cuddled in his arms. "I finally got Sandy to close her eyes for a little bit. We need you, Mom, we do, but not like this. Please, go with Brigitte, keep the appointment. We all have cell phones. We'll call the minute we hear anything." Oscar brought Martha over and set her gently in his mother-in-law's arms before pouring himself a cup of coffee. He leaned against the center island and held the cup against his cheek for a moment. Brigitte spread the last piece of toast with butter and jam and handed it to him before dropping a few more slices into the toaster.

Cecelia ran her finger lightly along Martha's cheek as she looked up at Oscar. "Are you sure about this? It'll probably take a few hours at least."

"Sandy and I will manage. Barring another storm, I'm off work until Tuesday, at least. Besides, Brigitte knows medicine. She'll be a good person to have in your corner for the appointment this morning." Just then, they heard the commode flushing upstairs, and Oscar looked pointedly at her. "Do it for Sandy, Mom, please? She can't . . ."

Cecelia held up her hand and gestured for Oscar to come and get the baby. "You're right. I'll go and get ready." Oscar took Martha and settled her against his shoulder, then reached the other hand out to help his mother-in-law from her chair. Once she was steady, he reached an arm around her and gave her a brief hug.

"Thank you," he said to Cecelia and then again to Brigitte as she closed up the loaf of bread and tucked it back into the spot on the counter where it belonged.

"I've got her, hon. You eat." Brigitte picked up Martha and stood rocking her gently while Oscar worked his way through two more pieces of toast. When Cecelia re-emerged, her pocketbook over her shoulder, Brigitte settled the baby in the nearby swing and pulled it over where Oscar could reach her if she needed anything. "Call us if you hear anything, okay?"

Oscar nodded at them, pouring coffee with one hand, the other resting gently on the edge of the baby swing. Brigitte touched her hand to his shoulder for a moment before reaching for Cecelia's arm and helping her out the door.

23

Before anyone went back into the church, Rod spoke with the two officers on the sidewalk near the blackened camera. They talked him through the steps they'd taken with the search the day before, repeating many of the details that Ms. Washington had given him about the fire drill. Then, Rod gestured toward the door. "What can you tell me about the emergency alarm for this door?"

The female officer pulled out an old-fashioned notepad and flipped to a page midway through it. "The emergency lock wasn't working, but no one could tell us how long it had been out. Apparently, one or two of the staff, as well as the Reverend, liked to duck out this door to have a smoke."

Rod pulled on the door, but from the outside, it remained locked. "Interesting, it's still locking even though the alarm isn't working. I guess that's why no one was concerned. Probably the sign was enough to discourage people from using it." He sent the other officer around to the backdoor to let them in while they waited. "What else did you notice about this area yesterday, the kitchen, laundry room?"

"There was food set out in the kitchen. It looked like lunch stuff with plastic plates and little cups all lined up. They were in the middle of feeding the kids when we got here."

"And the laundry room? What was in the cart?"

"The cart was empty, but there was a load in the washer when we got here. One of the staff," she checked her writing. "Mia, her name was. She said she'd started the washer. I guess the bedding gets pretty gross, sometimes."

Rod imagined the young woman emptying the cart, putting the items in the washer. "Was that standard procedure, do you know?"

"Yeah, the director told us everyone had access to this area, and they shared the responsibility for cleaning."

"Do the parents provide the sheets for the cribs?"

She shook her head. "No, the church uses white cotton ones that they can wash at high temperatures." She gestured at the table where Rod noticed that the towels, and everything else, were all white.

"What can you tell me about the missing baby's crib or carrier or whatever they put them in here?"

Again, she consulted her notes as the door opened, and they followed the second officer back inside. "The center has a crib for each baby, but everyone we talked to said that the twins liked to be together, so one of the cribs isn't used. That's why it took them a little while to realize that one of them was missing. The fact that they were both in purple confused things even more."

"How long do they say it took before anyone sounded an alarm?"

"The director said no more than fifteen minutes. She said she called the police and the parents. The police arrived here first, but the parents weren't far behind. I caught a ride with Detective Smith. We got here a little after eleven-thirty. He stationed one of us at each exit while they searched the building. They even brought in a dog, but nobody found anything."

"You said that you talked to a woman on the staff here named Mia, is that right?"

"Yes, just briefly, though, like I said. She was in the laundry room."

"How did she act? Did you get any impressions of her?"

The officer looked quizzically at him before consulting her notes again, but she folded it shut and shook her head. "I guess I didn't really, nothing that stood out. She seemed anxious; they all did. These are not high-paying jobs, and if the center closes, they'll all be out of work."

"They said that?"

"I heard it, too, detective," the other officer added. "They were already worried that they'd lose their certificate because of the fire drill. The director had warned them about it over and over. Once the press showed up yesterday, they all looked frightened."

"All right, thank you both. I appreciate your coming back out here."

"Is there anything else you need?"

Rod pulled his notebook out of his pocket and began writing. He looked up briefly. "Yeah, would you two count those sheets and then go and ask, see if there are any missing?" He paused. "Do me a favor, ask more than one person about the count, would you?"

As Rod leaned against the wall making his notes, the two young officers completed their count and then left the laundry room and headed back to the daycare area. He had little evidence to go on at this point, but an idea was beginning to form in his mind. It was remarkable how often the assistant Mia's name came forward whether they were talking to the parents or the staff. And today, she was the only one unaccounted for.

Soon the officers were back. "Sorry, detective, we asked a few people, but no one seemed to know for sure how many there should be."

The female officer added, "the assistant director found an inventory form, but it was so old, no one trusted what it said." He nodded and thanked the two for their help before all of them headed back out.

In his car on the way back to the station, Rod called Smitty, but when he didn't get an answer, he figured his partner was probably in another interview. Rod left a message telling him what he'd learned and then headed toward the address he'd gotten for Mia Novak's apartment. When he got there, he found the building a little more run-down than he'd been expecting. Although it was a weekday, the area seemed to be filled with people milling about or sitting in doorways. A bar around the corner from her apartment had its door open, and loud, country music was playing inside.

A chatty, busybody of a landlady led him up two flights of stairs to the apartment. When no one answered his knock, the woman pulled out a wad of keys and, on the fourth try, let him in. He called out again, announcing his name and police rank, before entering the small space. It looked clean, he thought. There was a kitchenette that seemed too small for anyone to cook in. He opened the door and found the refrigerator held a half-dozen eggs, a loaf of bread, some margarine, and most of a six-pack of beer.

"Hey, what the hell?" a young woman yelled, slamming her bag onto the small counter behind him.

Rod stood up quickly and pulled his badge from his pocket. "Detective Rodriguez, ma'am, Pittsburgh homicide."

"Homicide? Is someone dead? What are you doing in here?"

"No ma'am, sorry, I'm not working homicide today. I'm helping with a missing persons case. Are you Mia Novak?" He didn't think she matched the description he'd been given, but he wanted to be sure. He was relieved when the woman's tone moderated as she slipped from outrage to irritation.

"No, my name's Bethany, Bethany Hall. Mia's my roommate, or she's supposed to be at any rate."

"What do you mean?"

She spread her hands wide, indicating the rooms around her. "We were halfway through the month before she paid any rent. That landlady probably let you in here figuring it'd help her collect."

"So why hasn't Ms. Novak paid. She has a job, right?"

"Two jobs, actually."

"Two jobs?"

"Well yeah, she does the daycare thing in the morning, and then afternoons, she's been helping at her cousin's bar. It's just down the block." She jerked her hand over her shoulder to the left and then settled on the sofa. "What'd she do? Why are you here?"

"I need to talk to her. Something happened at the daycare center where she works, and I'm trying to follow up."

"Oh my God, I saw that on the news. I didn't realize that was the place that Mia worked. Man, she didn't even like that job." She laughed and raised her shoulders with an air of indifference. "I don't even think she likes kids very much."

Rod saw his theory of a young woman wanting a baby of her own sail right out the window. Back to square one. "When's the last time you saw her?"

"I dunno, last weekend maybe? She brought a guy home, and after he left, she told me she had another housesitting job lined up, so she'd be gone."

"Do you know who the guy was?"

"No, I didn't hear a name if she even said one. I only got a glimpse of him. He seemed older than her, though, probably some dude she met at the bar. It didn't look very serious." She paused then, leaning against the small counter. "You know, after that she did tell me that she was thinking about getting a place of her own."

"Really? How could she afford that if she's already struggling to pay on this place?"

The young woman shrugged again. "Beats me."

"Could I take a look at her room? I won't go in, I promise."

"Knock yourself out. Hers is the one on the right, the messy one."

He stood in the doorway of the bedroom and looked around. The room wasn't much larger than the bed, with an open closet bursting with clothes and a bedside table that sported an overflowing ashtray as well as a baggy that he guessed held weed. Without a warrant, Rod didn't feel comfortable looking at the apartment in any more detail, so he thanked the roommate and headed down the block to the cousin's bar.

Since the assistant director was on site that day, Smitty kept the director in the coffee room while he took his time interviewing the other staff. Coming to the station house today were two teachers and two out of the three part-time assistants. It wasn't a large staff, but from what he was learning, it was a much better adult-to-child ratio than many centers had. The teacher in charge of the toddlers was in her mid-fifties and had worked at the church and the daycare center for more than twelve years. The one for the babies' room, he wasn't quite sure why babies needed a teacher, but at any rate, she was a young woman in her first position since earning her degree in early childhood. He'd investigated the young woman's school record but found nothing of concern. The two assistants who'd been in were a Mutt and Jeff pair if he'd ever seen one. Shoshana was just seventeen and had been working for the summer only. She was heading to college in just a week and worried that the investigation would stop her from leaving. Mildred was the other end of the spectrum. At 72, she was a spry bundle of energy that belied her age in every way. She said she had tried retirement in her mid-sixties but hadn't liked it at all, so she'd begun working at the center about four years earlier. She had opinions about everyone on the staff as well as all the families and children. That interview had taken the longest, and Smitty had made lots of notes, but in the end, he wasn't sure how reliable the information might be.

Just before noon, he brought Miriam Bianchi, the director, back in. He noticed that her gray hair was still neatly in place, but her hands were rarely still as she constantly took her glasses off and put them back on, even while answering a single question. A quick look at everyone's financial records had made it clear to Smitty that no one was making much money from the center. With maintenance costs and liability insurance, the church itself barely seemed to break even. In his call with the Reverend, he'd sensed that it was a constant topic of conversation among the church's trustees.

Rod walked in and took a seat as Smitty continued his questioning. "Mrs. Bianchi, thank you for waiting. You've had some time to think back over the events yesterday. What do you believe happened?" Rod scooted his chair forward, and Smitty noticed how the sound made the woman flinch. She didn't seem like a crier to him, but she was definitely on edge. He waited for a few long moments as she continued to fiddle with her glasses.

Finally, she folded them and rested both hands in her lap. "I just don't know. I'm sorry. I spoke at length with the Reverend last night as well, and I just don't have an explanation."

"What can you tell us about the fire drill?" Rod asked.

"The fire drill?" Smitty thought she looked surprised by the question. "We did fine with it. Everyone was out in the allotted time, then I turned off the alarm, and we went back inside."

"Did you take roll or do any sort of checking once everyone was outside? Did you have any kind of list?"

"Well, no, not really. I just know everyone was there. I saw them."

"I was told that people were holding the babies and some of the toddlers. Who was holding who? Who had which baby?"

Both Rod and Smitty watched as the woman's face seemed to freeze for a moment. Smitty added, "take your time. Close your eyes if you need to and picture the scene outside."

"I know that two of the babies were in their carriers. Ronnell had one and was holding the hand of at least one toddler. She was at the head of the line as we went out."

"Good, now who was next?" Smitty leaned in a bit, encouraging her as she struggled to remember.

"Uh, I think there were two or three toddlers behind her. Mildred had another carrier and was ushering children ahead of her. Then there were a couple more. Uh, I think Shoshana was next. She was holding a baby and the hand of one of the smaller ones."

"And Mia?" Rod asked.

"Mia?" The woman looked from one detective to the other. Then something clicked. "Mia had a baby on her shoulder and her hands full of dirty bed linens. She handed the little one to me and then went and dropped things in the laundry room. She came running back before we were out the door, and I handed the baby I was holding back to her."

"Where were the twins, Mrs. Bianchi? Where were Martha and Rose when you all were outside?" Smitty asked the question, but both men held their breath as they waited.

At that, she broke, her face falling, tears overwhelming her, leaving her unable to speak. Rod handed her a tissue, but neither man offered a comment. Sobs hit her then, and she struggled to regain control. Finally, she whispered, "I can't remember. I should have had a list. I should have checked everyone off when we got outside."

That much was obvious to everyone, but it didn't seem like a productive line of thinking. Once she had regained a bit of control, Rod asked. "What can you tell us about Mia?"

"Mia? She's a good girl, always on time, hardly ever calls in sick." The director tilted her head to the side as she considered the question. "I wouldn't say that she was a natural with children, at least not with babies, but she always did what was expected."

"Did you ever have to discipline her?"

"Discipline? No, I've never had to discipline any of my staff."

"What about minor issues? There must have been some of those." Smitty continued to lean forward, unwilling to allow the director any more room to equivocate.

The woman lifted her arms in frustration. "She started back in the winter last year. At first, I had to scold her to put her phone away, but she got better about that. All I can think of now is the bathroom. Sometimes I had to shoo her back out of there."

"You think she was in there on the phone?"

"Sometimes maybe, but I also heard the water running a long time. I'm not sure Mia was entirely comfortable with the hygienic care that babies need."

Rod and Smitty exchanged looks before Rod offered a clarification. "She didn't like getting shit on her hands, is that what you're saying?"

Mrs. Bianchi dabbed at her eyes and nodded but said nothing more. When neither man had any more questions, Smitty walked her out to the front desk. Rod was on the computer again when he returned. "It all centers on Mia, doesn't it?" asked Smitty.

"Yep. I thought that maybe she was one of those women who's so crazy for babies that they take one. You hear about it happening in hospitals sometimes." Rod shook his head. "But she doesn't seem like the right sort. Even the roommate said she didn't think Mia liked kids very much."

"So why take one?" Smitty leaned back in his chair, absently scratching the edge of his scar.

"That's the big question, isn't it? Would she try and sell it for profit? Or take it for someone else? The roommate mentioned Mia bringing a guy home a while back, someone older than her. And, she said that Mia had mentioned getting a place of her own." He spread his hands out wide. "Hard to see where she'd get the funds for that. The second job she had was working at her cousin's bar. I talked with him for almost an hour, pushed as far as I could, but he hadn't seen her either. Could be she met someone there."

By this time, Rod had pulled up access to the young woman's finances. He leaned back so that Smitty could see over his shoulder. "That is pitiful. Look at how small those paychecks are. No wonder she needed a second job."

"Yep, and you'll notice that there are no paychecks from the bar at all. I'm guessing her cousin was paying Novak under the table."

"What kind of hours did she work there?"

Rod flipped back to his notes. "From what the cousin told me, he had her holding down the bar in the afternoons when it wasn't busy. She'd wait tables, fix the drinks. It wasn't exactly doing a booming business when I went by."

"You think she met someone there?"

"I don't know. The bottom line is, we don't know where she is."

"So, you're telling me we don't have just one missing person. We've got two." Smitty confirmed what Rod had been thinking.

"And a clock ticking on both of them, no doubt," Rod added. Both men stood and began collecting their things. "Listen, I'm going to go back to that bar, push the cousin some more now that the arrangement looks a little shadier. I'll see what I can find out about any men she might have met there."

"Sounds good. I'm going to go and check in with the captain, see how he wants to handle the situation with Mia. Call me if you hear anything."

"You got it." Rod paused, then looked at Smitty. "Do we say anything more to the family at this point?"

"I don't know. Let me check with the captain first. I'll let you know."

25

Saturday morning, the brightly blinking alarm woke Audrey from a deep sleep. She reached to turn it off as two thoughts collided at once. Relief and guilt. Guilt washed over her first. How could she have slept when Sandy and Oscar's baby had now been gone for two days? What kind of a friend was she? Then, relief rushed in as she realized she'd slept through the night without a single bad dream. At the contradiction, she buried her face in the pillow once more. She was a terrible person. There was no question about it. When the circle swung around to guilt again, she propelled herself out of bed and into the shower.

Once she was dressed and functioning on a few more cylinders, Audrey made coffee and checked her messages. She was disappointed to see that nothing had come through after Rod's quick note about missing dinner. The urge was so strong to call Rod or her mother, anyone who could tell her what was going on. But it wasn't the right thing to do. She knew it. Everyone was already doing what they could to find Rosey and pestering them wouldn't make their jobs any easier. She had work to do as well and began assembling her photography equipment so that she'd be ready for Katy's shower.

Three hours later, she was home, the din of the happy, all-female crowd still reverberating through her head. She set her camera bag and purse on the table and pulled the hearing aids out at once. She knew she'd need them later, but for now, the quiet was bliss. The noise had actually been a sign of how well the shower went, Audrey thought as she propped her feet up on the chair next to her, rubbing at the spots where the dress shoes had been biting into them. Sisters were something, she marveled, and then shook her head for a moment as she pictured Rosey and Martha sleeping side by side in their crib at home.

With a resolve she didn't feel, she turned to her email and noticed that it held a note from her mother. She'd taken Sandy's mom, Cecelia, to her doctor's appointment, and a date had been set for the first surgery. Three months later, if all went well, they would do the second. Audrey counted it off in her head and was pleased to think that maybe her friend's mom would be back in her painting studio by spring. Unfortunately, the other news was not so good.

Nothing more had been heard of Rosey, she reported, and Sandy and Oscar were growing despondent. Even Martha seemed to be feeling the loss and was having more trouble than usual, with both sleeping and eating. Neither Smitty nor Rod had been able to update them with new information. Audrey scanned the rest of her email, but when she didn't see anything from Rod, she decided to reach out. Perhaps there was more he knew that they weren't ready to share with the parents. She didn't want to disturb his work, though, so she kept the text brief. She thought about phoning Sandy but couldn't come up with a single thing to say. Besides, she told herself, just the call itself would probably be disturbing. Unable to sit still, she changed from her nice outfit into workout clothes and headed to the gym.

As she reached to open the outer door to her apartment building, the panic gripped her once again. Suddenly, she could see the hatred on Gary Adams's face as he attacked her, feel the pain in her head, the gun at her back, hear the hissed order to walk out the door. The taste of blood filled her mouth, and all of it washed over her in a matter of seconds as she gripped the doorknob and tried to move forward, her heart racing as she struggled to breathe. She jumped as the knob twisted in her hand, but it was just her neighbor, and she blushed at being caught in the panic. "How's it going?" she managed to stammer before stepping aside and then down the front steps. She sat down on the lowest one for a moment and waited for her heart rate to return to normal. God, she needed this trial to be over, for Adams to be back in jail permanently. She knew he was being held without bond, but it didn't lessen any of her fears. If she was going to get through all of this, she needed him to be in jail for good.

She forced herself to her feet once again and began walking toward the gym as the shakes finally began to fade.

An hour and a half later, she was back home, the workout having burned off some of the dread and worry. She felt her phone vibrating in her back pocket as she dropped her gym bag by the door and began toeing off her shoes. "Hey, Rod, you got my note. Is there any word on Rosey?" She couldn't help but ask the obvious.

"I'm sorry, no. I wish I had something more."

"And I'm sorry, I didn't even say hello first. How are you doing? How's Smitty?"

"We're both okay, just frustrated like everyone else. That's one reason I was calling you. So far, we haven't found the daycare worker that Oscar and Sandy seemed to know the best. She had a second job bartending downtown, and I was wondering if you'd like to come and check it out with me. We could get some dinner afterward if you're free."

"That'd be great. I need to get a quick shower first. Can you come get me in about thirty?"

"Sure, I'll be over. Thanks, Scout."

She was waiting on the front steps when he pulled up. She figured it couldn't hurt to try some desensitization training, so she'd stepped outside a little bit early and then stood there, working to hold her breathing even and block out the panicked thoughts. The bottom line was that she was either going to get past this fear or have to look for a new place to live. It was as simple and as complicated as that. She was relieved to see Rod pull up. She climbed in the passenger door and reached to hug him for a moment before settling into her seat and buckling her belt.

Rod grinned, happy to see her in spite of the task they were headed out on. "How's it going with the front door today?"

Audrey leaned back in her seat, brushing her bangs back off her forehead. "Embarrassingly bad, I'm afraid. I almost screamed earlier when my neighbor came in right as I was going out."

"Hey now, c'mon, you've got to give yourself a break, you know. It takes time to process something as traumatic as what you went through. I think you're being too hard on yourself." He reached over and held her hand before pulling out into the stream of traffic.

"Thanks, I know what you're saying, but I still feel like a big baby. I just wish I didn't." She shrugged. "So, where are we going again?"

"For now, there's no news, no ransom note or call. There's also no sign of Mia Novak, the assistant from the center."

"What do you know about her?"

"Not a whole lot. She has a roommate, but I don't think they get along very well. She takes jobs pet sitting and housesitting, so she's away from the apartment a lot. She has a second job bartending for her cousin in the afternoons, but he hasn't seen her either, not since Wednesday afternoon."

"Are you thinking she took Rosey?"

"We're struggling with that. It seems likely, but from what we've been told, Mia didn't have much of an affinity for babies."

"Even though she worked in a daycare?"

"Yeah, I mean everyone said she did her job fine, but she didn't really seem to like babies all that much, hated cleaning up after them especially. A little germophobic even, to hear the director tell it."

"Does that mean she took her to hurt her? I don't understand."

"Smitty and I are thinking that maybe she took her for someone else, perhaps to sell? We're not sure." By this time, they had reached the area of the bar, and Rod pulled into a parking spot halfway down the block. He gestured at the building ahead of them on the corner. "So that building is where her apartment is, upstairs." Then he leaned against the window and gestured behind them in the other direction. "That's the cousin's bar. Let's head in there and see if anyone has seen or heard from her. I want to grill the cousin a little more too."

Once inside, they gave their eyes a minute to adjust to the gloom. Despite the sunshine outdoors, inside, it was both dark and loud. Television sets of various ages and sizes circled the two rooms that made up the bar's interior. Most were tuned to the afternoon's baseball game, but one lone set in the back was showing golf. To Audrey, it didn't seem as though anyone was watching the sets, but a quick cheer and then booing told her she was wrong. She and Rod made their way through the maze of tables and found seats near the end of the bar. However, it took several minutes before the busy bartender acknowledged them.

"You're back, huh? What can I get you?" The man looked to be in his early fifties and was wiping the bar and setting glasses in the small sink at the same time.

Rod lifted the empty bowl in front of him and said, "Two beers and a few more peanuts if you've got them."

"Sure thing," he nodded and turned toward the swinging door to the kitchen where a young man in a wool cap was bringing out a plastic tray filled with clean plates and bowls. "Get the big bag of peanuts, would you?" The young man took his time stacking the clean dishes and collecting the nearly filled bus bin before heading back through the swinging door. The bartender tossed down two paper coasters and then set their drinks in front of them.

"Any word yet from Mia?" Rod asked after nodding his thanks for the drink.

"Nah, and I could use her today, that's for sure."

"When did you see her last?" Rod took a sip and waited for the bartender to take an order from one of the overworked servers.

He talked as he pulled the taps to fill the various glasses. "Like I told you before. I haven't seen her since Wednesday when she finished her shift and sat down to have a bite of dinner. Now I've got work to do."

"Hey." There was a hardness to Rod's voice that had the bartender whipping his head back around. "How many employees you paying under the table here? Do we need to get the IRS involved? Maybe a health inspector?"

The man leaned heavily on the bar, jutting his chin toward Rod. "Look, Mia's family, all right? I'm worried about her. Yeah, I paid her under the table. She never made more than a couple hundred a week. Everyone else is on the books. You want to report me? Go ahead."

He turned away then, slapping at the swinging door as he disappeared into the kitchen. Rod turned back to Audrey. "It was worth a shot, I figured. He's Mia's cousin."

"You seen Mia?" The young man had returned, an enormous bag of peanuts in his arms.

"You know her? What's your name?" Rod asked as he began filling several small wooden bowls.

"Carlos, Carlos Santiago. Sure, I know her." He looked toward the kitchen, but once the bartender was out of sight, he added, "She's hot!"

"You were seeing her?" Rod asked, and Audrey wondered about the age gap that would have been in play.

The young man seemed a little embarrassed. "Nah, I wish, though, you know, but she was out of my league."

"When did you see her last?" Audrey noticed Rod leaning slightly, trying to will information out of the young man.

Carlos finished filling the bowls and began setting them up on the bar before wrapping the top of the bag closed and fastening an old clothespin around it. "I guess it was Wednesday when she worked last, but I also saw her for a second, uh, Thursday night, I think it was, pretty late."

Rod and Audrey exchanged a quick look. "Thursday night, you're sure? Was she working?"

"Nah, man, it was late, like real late. I was supposed to be gone by then, but I forgot my phone in the kitchen and had to come back in and get it."

"What was she doing?"

"She was with this dude, man, but he was not good enough for her, way too old. I mean, no offense, but like maybe even older than you."

"Were they drinking?"

"I think he had been, but she just walked in through the kitchen and then walked him back out the same way."

"Did you see where they went?"

"Nah, man, like I said. I was supposed to be home by then. My mom was already mad that I had to go back out. Mia just said hi as I was leaving."

"Do you know the man's name?"

"I'm trying to think." He held the peanut bag against him, his eyes looking up through a fringe of dark hair as he considered the question. "Nah, sorry." He lowered his gaze. "I think I might have heard her call him Jewels or something, but that doesn't make any sense. Sorry man, I got nothing."

Rod reached over the bar and shook his hand. "Thanks. I appreciate you talking with me."

"Will you let me know when you find her? I'm kind of worried, you know?"

"Will do. I'll be in touch with your boss, too." The young man ducked his head briefly in thanks and then returned to the kitchen.

"I'm guessing by the look on your face that this is news, right?" Audrey asked.

"It's the first time, the only time anyone has mentioned seeing her on Thursday after the police were at the center."

"And the guy, Jewels, sounds like a nickname, not much to go on."

"Well, if I can get a warrant to see the bar's receipts for the last month or so, it might tell me something. Let's get out of here."

Rod laid a twenty on the bar and then led the way back through the tables. Once outside, though, instead of heading toward the car, he led Audrey down the side of the building toward the alley in back. "Let's take a look while we've still got some light."

Audrey studied the side of the building as they walked, but nothing seemed to stand out. There were a few scattered beer cans, most of them rusted and bent in half. At the back of the building, there was a weedy, overgrown area with some scrubby trees and a battered old picnic table in its center. The table and ground all around it were covered with cigarette butts. She looked up at Rod. "Did Mia smoke?"

"Yeah, I think I saw an ashtray near her bed, as a matter of fact. Looked like weed and cigarettes."

"Do you think they came back here to smoke?" The two of them looked around them, Rod's gaze seemed to focus on the alley, but Audrey leaned against the end of the picnic table and looked at the ground around her. The table was resting on a concrete pad that was chipped and broken in several places, but a dark stain near one corner caught her eye. "Rod." She motioned for him to come closer. "Look at this."

Rod crouched down and parted the weeds, looking carefully at the stained area. Without a word, he pulled out his phone and hit speed dial. It was picked up quickly. "Smitty, we need a warrant for the cousin's bar. We need to see their receipts for the last two months, and we need to search the area behind it. Audrey's here, so have someone bring the camera." Audrey couldn't hear what the response was, but he grunted and ended the call quickly. "Good eye, Scout."

"Do you think it's blood?"

Rod nodded and crouched down once again, his hands indicating the area that the stain covered. "I think it's a lot of blood, actually. I may be wrong. It may turn out someone just dumped a bunch of wine back here, but I don't think so."

Although it was Saturday, Julius was happy to be back at work. The company rotated their computer repair experts through a schedule that required each technician to work one weekend a month. This one was his, and he was happy to have an excuse to leave the house and do work that could take his mind off the situation. After parking in the empty lot, he unlocked the service door and flipped on lights as he made his way into the large room. He put his sandwich into the fridge in the employee area and then headed to his desk. While his computer booted up, he took a few minutes to start a pot of coffee. He discovered that whoever had made it last hadn't cleaned up properly and was pissed that he was forced to wash everything first before loading up the fresh grounds and starting it to heat—lazy shits.

Back at his desk, his email contained only half a dozen tickets for work that were needed. That was a relief and a workload that he didn't think would take him more than two or three hours. Depending on what came in after, he might finish early and have time to stop by the bar on his way home. He pictured Mia standing behind the counter pulling a pint for him and had to drop his head down into his hands. God, how had everything gone so wrong?

The coffee pot dinged, so he got up and poured a cup, doubling the flimsy cups to manage the heat. With the coffee in hand, he took a few minutes to walk around. During the week, every cubicle was occupied, and the air filled with dozens and dozens of conversations. With everyone gone and the room nearly silent, he took his time studying the various photos and tchotchkes that cluttered everyone's desk. There were lots of baby photos he noticed, although none of them looked as pinched and miserable as the one at his house.

Hannah had been amazing so far, he thought, holding and rocking the screaming child, getting up in the night without complaint, but it was definitely wearing on him. Just like the day before, his emotions swung from being angry at Mia for grabbing a sick kid and then feeling guilty and despondent over what he'd done to her. He'd never meant to hurt her, that was for sure. In fact, he'd been looking forward to keeping their affair going. He sipped at his coffee and returned to his workstation.

Work trickled in throughout the day, so he wasn't able to get away early as he had planned. It was still light, though, when he headed home. He took the long way, letting himself settle into the evening's stream of cars. In no rush to get anywhere, he waited patiently as the lanes stopped and started, weaving in and around each other in a familiar rhythm. He was in front of Mia's bar before he noticed the direction he'd gone, and the urge to go in was almost overwhelming. But he imagined the questions that he might face and, instead, drove past and continued toward home. There was a liquor store on the way, so he stopped in there and picked up a bottle before returning home. He pulled the car into the garage and closed the door. There was no need for the stolen vehicle to be any more noticeable than it already was. He wondered if the person with the car lot had discovered the switch yet and struggled to think what he should do about that situation.

He opened the door into the kitchen, bracing himself for the screams that he expected to hear. But there was nothing. "Hannah?" He called out. "Where are you?" He walked into the kitchen and then through on into the living room. There were a couple of empty baby bottles on the coffee table but no sign of his wife. Panic started to grab at his midsection. He took the stairs two at a time and went into the bedroom and bath, but there was no one. The door to the nursery was ajar, and he pushed it open, expecting to see Hannah conked out in the rocker, the baby asleep in the crib. But both were empty.

He barreled back down the stairs and hit speed dial on his phone. He listened to it ring and ring before Hannah's voicemail message began to play. A shockingly syrupy tone played a new message "Hannah and little Joy are unable to take your call." Just then, the garage door began rising, its motor quiet but distinctive. He heard a crash, then something metal falling to the ground. He wished he had a gun of some kind, a weapon of any sort that he could wield against an intruder. He dashed into the kitchen and began to pull the largest knife out of the block when he heard Hannah's distinctive laugh. He dropped the knife back into its place and leaned against the counter. Calm down, for fuck's sake, he told himself. What is your problem? He yanked a paper towel off the roll, ripping and leaving a full third of it behind. Fear spiked into anger, and he reached to throw the towels and the metal base that held them across the room. But Hannah's face appeared, a broad smile spreading as she spotted him, so he used the towel to wipe the flop sweat from his neck before moving forward to greet her.

"Where were you? I was worried." He heard the garage door closing as he held the inner door open and helped her lift the stroller inside, forcing himself to smile. He hadn't known that they even owned a stroller.

"Hi, honey." She kissed him on the cheek before setting the brake and then lifting out the child. In sleep, the baby looked more normal, he thought. "We were just having a walk around the neighborhood. The movement seemed to calm her down and look. She's fallen asleep. Here, why don't you hold her while I get dinner going?"

Julius went rigid as she placed the warm, sweaty infant in his arms. "No, what? I can't . . ."

"Of course, you can. Now just come and sit here at the table, and I'll keep an eye on you both." Hannah put her hand on his back and gave a slight push before pulling the chair out in front of him.

He moved, finally, but sat down stiffly and continued to hold the child away from his body. The baby stirred, but luckily, she didn't wake. A new panic hit him then at the idea of them strolling around the neighborhood when the news of the kidnapping was still so fresh. "Hannah, did you see anyone you knew? Did you talk to anyone on your walk today?"

She was busy pulling leftovers out of the refrigerator but turned to look at him. The smile still covering her face. "I was hoping I would. I especially wanted to see the people who live behind us since our yards meet up. They have a little girl, too. But they were just leaving in their car when I went by, so all I could do was wave."

Relief washed over him then, and he rested his arms in his lap, allowing the baby's weight to settle onto his legs. It wasn't a bad sensation, he thought, as he studied the sleeping infant. He could hear Hannah humming as she went about putting dinner together for them, could feel the pleasure that she was finding in the experience. But to Julius, it was as if the three of them were sitting on a raft at the edge of a storm, calm and peaceful at the moment, but with danger waiting silently on the horizon.

"You were right. Let's get some photographs before we start digging around in this area." Behind the bar, Rod nodded to the technician, sent Smitty a quick text, and then watched as the rest of the forensics team began unloading equipment. One of them handed Audrey the department camera, and she went to work recording the scene.

Once they were busy getting set up with lights and a folding table, Rod conferred with the technician again, his arm indicating a line to his left. "We think there might be a blood trail leading down this way toward the alley. I was looking for tire tracks but couldn't get a read on anything definitive."

"Yeah, looks a mess, lots of trucks and cars in and out, I'm guessing." The man turned back to his team, and Rod stepped out of the way. He had pulled his car around back to help block off the alley, so he leaned against the driver's door now as he watched Audrey and the rest of the team work. He pulled out his phone and reviewed the details they had on Mia from the daycare center director. There were fingerprints on file, but the emergency card was incomplete, and Rod was frustrated to find that it did not list a blood type. A second vehicle pulled up behind his, and he went over to greet Smitty and bring him up to date.

"Hey man, what's the word?" Rod asked as he gripped Smitty's hand, and the two of them stepped a bit closer to the area cordoned off with bright yellow caution tape.

"The judge was waiting for us to confirm that what you found was blood. Once we knew that, he signed off on both warrants."

"I'm thinking the cousin is not too happy with me right now since I made him shut down for the night. I've got a uniform inside sitting on him and the busboy. You want to head in and serve him with the warrant for the receipts, get a read on him yourself?"

"Sure thing."

Rod watched as Smitty tucked his shirttail in and then pulled on a lightweight jacket with the city's police logo on the back of it. He folded his badge into the jacket pocket and then reached into the car and pulled out the paperwork. With a quick salute, he walked around the crew and along the side of the building to the front. Rod pulled out his small notebook and began taking down the details from the back of the bar. Once she finished, Audrey came over and leaned against the car beside him. "What are they saying, Scout?"

"It's blood for sure, and at least one of the team members said it's a lot."

"How much is a lot?"

"They won't say until they've done more digging and collected more samples, but my sense was enough for it to have killed someone. They're speculating that someone hit their head on the corner of the cement pad. They think that's most likely the point of origin."

"Do they have a blood type?"

"Yeah, O positive. Pretty common, I'm afraid." Rod nodded but entered the information into his notes anyway. He didn't think it would be enough for a judge to allow them access to Mia's health records. After all, anyone could have been back behind the bar. It was just his gut that was telling him it was Mia.

Two hours later, everyone was finally packed up, and Rod and Audrey were able to go to dinner. They weren't in the mood for a fancy restaurant anymore, though, so they opted for takeout and headed through the tunnel out to Rod's house. They left their grimy shoes near the front door and dropped together onto the fat, leather sofa.

"God, I'm beat and starving."

"You and me both. What's your schedule tomorrow? Can you stay?"

Audrey leaned over to kiss him, lingering in the warmth and need that seemed to flow out of each of them. "I'm due at noon for a one o'clock wedding at the Heinz Chapel. What about you?"

He raised his hands in a gesture of uncertainty. "Who knows? I'm supposed to be off duty, just like today, but until we have an answer about Rosey, I don't think I'm going to relax."

"Rod, be honest. Do you think she's still alive?"

Rod took his time answering, rubbing her fingers between his hands as he considered the grim statistics that he knew he could be quoting. "I don't know, Audrey. I don't have a sense one way or the other. We still don't have any idea why Mia would have taken her. If it was to sell her, then yeah, she probably is alive . . ."

"But we may not be able to find her? Is that what you're thinking?"

He shrugged. "It's hard to know what to think. We're not giving up, though. No one is giving up. You can count on that." He stood and pulled her up next to him, holding her close for a moment before stepping back and picking up the plastic bag of takeout. "Come on. We need food. It's nearly nine."

Together they pulled out plates and utensils and set them on the table. Rod held up a bottle, but Audrey shook her head. "Sorry, I don't feel much like a beer tonight." Rod put it back in the fridge and got out two glasses that he filled at the tap.

"I'm with you, I guess. I don't think we'll get called out tonight, but why risk it?"

Once they were settled at the table, Audrey's thoughts returned to the upcoming trial. "Rod, have you been to a lot of trials? I've only been at one or two and not for long, so I'm wondering what to expect."

"Are you getting nervous?"

"I am feeling kind of sick, to be honest about it. I wish I didn't have to testify. I'm so afraid I'll mess up."

"What's to mess up?" He rested his hand on her arm. "You just have to tell the truth. You're the one who was there, who experienced it."

"But what if the jury doesn't believe me?"

Rod turned in his seat to face her squarely. "All right, tell me a lie. Big or small, it doesn't matter. Just tell me a lie."

Audrey looked at his face, puzzled by the demand. "Uh, I don't know. Watermelon is my favorite food."

"Not, I can see it in your face."

Audrey laughed. "You're right. It's cantaloupe. But what does that prove?"

"Just that I don't think you *could* tell a convincing lie, and the jury is going to see that. You have an honest face, an honest way of approaching the world, and the jury will respond to that, I'm sure. I'm just sorry I can't be there with you until after my testimony.

'Oh, I forgot, I was supposed to call my dad."

"Go ahead, why don't you step out on the back porch and talk while I clean this up?" Audrey stood and kissed Rod, and he pulled her in close. He hated to break away, but he knew she needed to make the call. "It'll be okay. You're dad's a good guy. Go and talk to him."

"Hi Dad, do you have a minute?" He closed the door behind her to give her a little bit of privacy and went about taking care of the kitchen mess. For a moment, he wished again that Simon was there with him, leaning against his leg and generally getting in the way.

CHAPTER

28

Audrey had photographed several weddings at the chapel, but the beauty of it never dimmed. They had taken lots of shots on the grounds after the service, and she knew they would be stunning. Then, once they'd completed those, the group had shifted to the University Club for the reception. Held on the expansive terrace upstairs with the city laid out below them, Audrey couldn't help but enjoy herself. With so much exciting architecture to work around, it would have been a crime for Audrey *not* to get the photographs right.

More than the sheer joy of the wedding, though, was the relief of doing something she loved instead of worrying about Rosey and the trial. She almost hated to see the wedding end, the couple taking off in a vintage pickup truck that had been decorated within an inch of its life. Audrey packed up her equipment and said a last goodbye to the bride's sister, who had helped her coordinate the photography. Then she was headed home, the ride dropping her off more quickly than she'd expected. At least she didn't feel the same sort of panic when she came back home that she often did when she left.

She took her time putting all of her equipment away before moving around the rest of the room to tidy it up before her father got there. She'd decided that she didn't want to be talking to him about everything in a restaurant, so she'd invited him for dinner instead. Once everything was straight, she ducked into the shower. Afterward, it felt good to put on an old t-shirt and jeans. Odd how clothes could make you feel sometimes. Her dressy work clothes made her feel alert and professional, while old jeans just felt like home somehow. She slipped her feet into her favorite flip-flops and got to work on dinner.

She was pleased that her apartment smelled of roasting chicken and garlic when her dad arrived. Of course, she'd had to crank up the AC a bit since it wasn't oven weather, but she didn't mind. She did envy Rod with his house and porch, though, and felt a bit wistful knowing it would take years of building her wedding photography business before she'd ever come close to owning a house.

"Hey, Dad," Audrey opened the door and fell into his welcoming hug.

"Hi, Audie, how are you doing? You've got your mom and me a little worried."

"Oh, Dad, I didn't mean to worry you guys. Come on in. Would you like a beer or some wine?"

"I'll have a glass of wine. It smells great in here."

Audrey brought him the glass as well as one for herself and settled beside him on the sofa. Dinner was ready, but it would keep while they talked. "First, Dad, tell me how everyone's doing. How are mom and Cecelia?"

"I think everyone over there is a bit of a wreck if you ask me. Your mom is helping a lot, though, making sure there's food for everyone and helping Cecelia especially."

"Is Oscar going to have to go back to work Monday morning?"

"I'm afraid so. I'm not sure he'd feel comfortable doing that if your mom wasn't helping."

"She didn't have any trouble getting out of her work?"

"No, she's started cutting back on her hours at the clinic anyway, so it wasn't hard for her to arrange." He paused, looking at her expectantly. "I take it there's no news, just between you and me and Rod?"

"There are a few leads, but I'm really not allowed to say anything, and I definitely don't want to get anyone's hopes up."

"So, the chances are bad. Is that what you're saying?"

Audrey took a sip of her wine before answering. "It's hard to say. For sure, the statistics are terrible. I think everyone knows that, but it's hard because no one knows why she was taken."

"Well, I know Rod and his partner are doing all they can, and that's *not* the reason I'm here. So, what's going on, Audie, and how can I help?"

"You know what, Dad, just coming here to dinner is a help, so thank you. There's something I haven't told you and mom, but now that the trial's coming up, I have to. I went to see a counselor yesterday, someone from victim's services."

He rested his hand on her knee. "Oh, honey, it tears me up to think of you in those terms."

"I know, Dad, but the truth is I *am* a victim, and I need help. I've been having panic attacks ever since it happened. And lately, with the trial coming up, they've gotten a lot worse."

"But why didn't you say anything?" He leaned back in order to study her face better. "You could have come home, stayed with us. We could have arranged for counseling there."

"I know, Dad, I thought the best way to deal with it was to get back to work, to my regular life and my business. I just didn't realize how hard that would be."

"Well, what did the counselor have to say?"

"She asked about my support network, and I realized that I needed to be honest with you because I think this week, I'm going to have to lean heavily. I know mom is needed at Sandy's, but would you be able to sit next to me during the trial? Rod has to testify as a witness, so he won't be allowed in until after he's finished."

"I haven't been subpoenaed. Am I supposed to testify?"

Audrey shook her head and took her dad's hand in hers. "No, Gabriel Perez, the lawyer, said there are enough witnesses from the scene in your neighborhood that they won't need to call you."

"Well, I'd be happy to speak if they needed me, but if they don't? Then yeah, I'm all yours. I'm in your corner for the long haul."

"And your job? Can you get away? I don't know how many days it will last."

"Honey, family comes first, period. And besides, I'm the boss now, and one skill I have developed is the ability to delegate. Like I said, I'm yours. What do I need to know?"

Audrey leaned over and rested her head against her dad's shoulder. She had known what his response would be, so why had she hesitated to tell him? She felt him lean over and kiss her on the top of the head. Then she looked up. "Why don't I feed you and tell you what I know so far?"

"Sounds good to me, honey. It smells delicious."

It took most of dinner to talk over what Gabriel had shared about his expectations for the trial. The fact that Adams's lawyer planned to focus his case on destroying Audrey's credibility made it especially hard to discuss. Since only Audrey had been present in the apartment when Adams assaulted her, the defense planned to characterize it as something very different from what it was.

"What's hard for me to handle is the fact that since I've recovered from the physical attack, it may be hard for the jurors to understand how bad it was."

Her dad set his fork down. "There are pictures, though, of how you looked, right? My God, I couldn't believe it when I saw you. Even days after the attack, your mom and I were still worried about the long-term effects you'd experience."

"It's kind of screwed up that the fact that I did recover physically somehow makes the case a little harder. That's why I wanted to tell you about the panic attacks. Gabriel is going to mention them as part of his prosecution."

Audrey's dad reached out and took her hand in his. "That's hard, isn't it, having something that feels private like that shared with a courtroom full of strangers?"

Audrey nodded and took a sip of her wine before replying. "It sucks, all of it sucks, and there's nothing I can do except face it head-on."

"Well, honey, I know for a fact that you can do that. I still remember the first day you had to go to school with the hearing aids. Your mom and I were so worried, so sure that you'd be teased and hassled about them, but you handled it. We were so proud of you."

"God, it was a horrible day, though." She shook her head, remembering the whispers and stares. "There was so much teasing, but Sandy stood by me, and that helped a lot."

"You know she feels bad that she can't be there for you now. She told your mom that. She hates letting you down."

"Oh, Dad, she shouldn't feel like that. I want to cry for poor Rosey, and I'm not even her mother. I can't imagine what Sandy and Oscar are going through. I'll give her a call tonight and make sure that she knows I understand."

"I think she'd like that, honey. Well," he stood and pushed his chair under the table before picking up his plate. "Let me help with the clean-up, and then I'll be off."

Audrey stood, took his plate, and set it on the counter before turning into him for one more hug. "I've got the cleanup, Dad. It's the least I can do to thank you for all of this."

He hugged her one more time before reaching for his keys and moving toward the door. "If you're sure, then I'll meet you Tuesday at 3:15 at the counselor's office, okay?"

"Okay, Dad, drive safely and give mom a big hug for me."

"Will do. Don't forget to make that call to Sandy, either. Both of you will feel better if you do."

Once he'd gone, Audrey threw the deadbolt shut and then got out her phone to call Sandy. Dishes could wait.

Monday morning, Rod was working at his desk, reviewing video footage from around the city, when a call came in from a detective in Zone Six. "Listen, the manager of the power plant on Brunot Island called and said one of their employees crossing the river on the railroad bridge spotted what looked to be a body down near the bridge's foundation. Our guys are pulling it in now, and the word is it's a young woman. I saw your missing person's report. You want in?"

"Definitely. I'm on my way." Rod ducked into the captain's office as soon as he put the phone down. "Cap, a detective just called to say that they think they have a body under the bridge near Brunot Island. Okay if I head out there? Word is it might be a young woman."

"Ah, Jesus, you think it's the daycare gal?"

"Don't know. I'd like to give our photographer a call and have her come with us. If this baby case goes to trial, we're going to want photos for sure."

"Good idea. Listen, take Smitty, too, would you? I think he's going nuts sitting at that desk."

"You got it." Rod dialed Audrey as he swept up his keys. "Audrey, it's Rod. Did you tell me you're on call today?"

"Yeah, today and tomorrow. What's up?"

"We think we might have a body out on the river."

"Oh, God, it isn't Rosey, is it?"

He could hear the hitch in her voice. "No, no, no, it might be a young woman, though, so I want to get a look and take some pictures. You free?"

"Yep, I can be there in ten unless you want to pick up the gear and come by. Are you in a hurry?"

"No, ten is fine. I'm going to see if I can grab Smitty too. See you in a few."

Rod said goodbye and clicked off before heading down the hall to Smitty's desk, where his partner seemed to be reviewing video footage as well. Apparently, they were both spinning their wheels this morning. "Smitty, Captain said for you to come with me. We've got a dead body, possibly a young woman, out by Brunot Island near the bridge."

"Gladly. Damn, I'm sick of sitting in this chair getting nowhere. The daycare center director told me they collect fingerprint records for all their employees, so that might help."

"Audrey should be here soon. You got any boots or wet gear?"

"Yeah, in my car. Let me go change, and I'll be right with you."

The three of them met a few minutes later and opted to go out in Rod's truck. They crossed the river to get to the other precinct house, but the boat hadn't returned with the body yet. "How do people get out to the power plant, Rod? They don't all take boats, do they?" Audrey asked.

"Nah, there's a walkway for them on the railroad bridge. That's where someone was when they saw it."

"I've never heard of that. Can anyone go over that way? Is there much on the island?"

"I'm not sure what's out there besides the power plant. I do know that cars have to take a ferry to get over, though." Smitty added.

They pulled into the lot at the precinct but didn't stay there long. The detective who had called offered to give them a ride down to the riverside where they would be meeting the police boat and the divers. Rod and Audrey climbed into the back seat while Smitty rode shotgun. It wasn't far, just a matter of weaving around the larger streets before they were able to pull up alongside the river not far from the railway bridge.

Rod leaned over to Audrey and asked in a whisper. "Are you okay with this? Bodies from the river can be incredibly awful."

"It's okay. My first call was to a drowning north of here on the river."

"Fresh is different, though. I just wanted to warn you."

"Thanks, I'll do my best. Camera up," she gestured.

"You got it."

The police boat that had collected the body was pulled up onto the bank near the railroad bridge. The body, not yet bagged for transport, looked about like Rod expected. There was some sort of jacket caught around the waist, the zipper hooked and snagged on what looked like old jeans. Her top, if she'd been wearing one, had been swept away, leaving a maze of meandering tattoo lines that circled the small breasts. Blond hair hung lank and weedy around the face. It looked as if the eyes might have been blue, but it was hard to tell. He heard Audrey snapping photos and hoped she'd be all right. "How long you think she's been in the water?" Rod asked the diver standing crouched next to him.

"Several days, I'd guess. Less than a week probably, or there'd be more animal damage than we see here. You think she's your missing person?"

The medical examiner arrived then, and Rod waited as the older man studied the slight body. As he lifted the head, Rod leaned over to get a better look and asked, "What do you see?"

"Looks to me like a nasty head wound. We'll have to see if there's water in the lungs. If I had to make a guess, though, I'd say it looks to me like a dump job."

Rod looked over at Smitty. "You think it's her?"

Smitty pulled up the photo of Mia Novak that the director had provided, but the smiling young woman bore little resemblance to the body lying in front of them now. "Hard to say. As soon as we've got some prints, we can run a comparison. Do you know when that will be?" He asked the M.E.

"Probably early this afternoon. It shouldn't take long once we get her back to the lab. You think you have enough photos?" He asked Audrey as they rolled the body back over.

"I think so. Are there any from the scene that we need?"

The detective who had brought them shook his head. "Nah, the divers took a few shots before they pulled her out. We're good."

Rod, Smitty, and Audrey stepped back away from the riverbank as the body was bagged and loaded into the M.E.'s van. The driver waved an imaginary hat as the rest of the crew departed in the boat.

As they drove back to the Sixth's precinct lot, the detective asked, "Does the head wound fit with your missing person's case?"

"If what we're thinking happened," Smitty answered, "yes. Once we've got the blood type and fingerprints, we'll know more. We appreciate the call."

"Hey, no problem. Happy to turn her over to you guys anyway. Nasty business ending up in that river."

He headed inside, and once Rod, Smitty, and Audrey were in the car headed back to their own precinct, the speculation began.

"Does this mean we're closer or farther away from finding Rosey?" Audrey asked.

"It's too soon to say." Smitty looked to the back seat, where Audrey was leaning forward.

Rod hated to see her get her hopes up. "Audrey, there's so much we don't know at this point. It will probably take time for us to be sure about the body, and even if this does turn out to be Mia Novak, and it turns out that the blood behind the bar is a match, we still don't have much more than a nickname to go on to find the guy she was with." He could see her shoulders deflate as she leaned back against the seat and looked out the open window. He regretted now that she'd been the photographer on call, hated that his work had made her life so much harder. He spoke softly, "You know you can't say anything to Sandy and Oscar, right?" He caught Smitty's eyes on him as he pulled into the lot.

Audrey got out, pulling the heavy camera equipment with her. She slung a bag over each shoulder and then reached up to kiss Rod on the cheek. "I know, Rod. I get it, and I appreciate getting the call out today. I just hope we get a break soon, that's all."

"Amen to that," Smitty added as they all made their way inside.

Monday evening, Julius was just getting onto the freeway when the local news broke through the music with a special report. "A body found this morning on Brunot Island has now been identified as Ms. Mia Novak, a childcare assistant from the center where infant Rose Wilder-Jones was abducted late last week. Cause of death has . . ." He snapped off the radio and clutched the steering wheel, his knuckles white. The road blurred before him for a moment as he pictured Mia smiling up at him in her bed and then staring blank faced as the blood pooled beneath her head. A horn blasted suddenly beside him, and he whipped the car back into his lane. Luckily an accident seemed to be slowing the traffic ahead, so he took his foot off the gas and allowed the car to slow. He leaned over to reach into the glovebox for the tissues Hannah kept there before he remembered that it wasn't his car. "Shit!" He slammed both palms against the wheel. How did they identify her so quickly, he wondered?

As the traffic ahead of him came to a complete stop, he waited and then followed four other vehicles as they snaked their way through the blocked lanes to the nearby exit ramp. It took two signal cycles before the long line could turn from the ramp onto the surface street. He didn't know the neighborhood at all, but the flashing neon signs from a pair of bars caught his eye. He pulled into the emptier of the adjacent lots and parked. Once inside, it was brighter than Mia's bar, so he grabbed a table near the back. It looked as though the after-work crowd was beginning to arrive, and he saw lots of pairs and larger groups meeting up at the bar and filling in the tables between him and the door. Panic started to hit him, drops of sweat making their way down his collar. "What can I get you?"

He was startled as an older woman, her uniform stained from years of wear, slapped a paper coaster on the table in front of him. "Let me have a whiskey, a double, and a beer chaser."

"You want something to eat with that?" He thought she looked at him suspiciously, and he hesitated in responding, wondering how she could know what he'd done. But when he looked up at her again, he noticed she wasn't even looking at him anymore. Instead, her attention caught on a loud group just entering the bar.

"Yeah, some fries." He pushed out the words, holding his breath until she'd stepped away. The television above the bar was showing a replay of a ball game, so he lowered his gaze, relieved that the news about Mia wasn't blaring in there as well. Inside his head, he screamed "Fuck!" loud and long, letting the word circle his brain again and again until the waitress reappeared with the drinks and a small bowl of some sort of snack mix. He downed the shot, then drank the beer as he systematically ate his way through the bowl, one item after the other without tasting any of it. When the fries came, he ordered another shot and a second beer and tried to force himself to slow everything down. He poured ketchup onto the edge of the plate and picked up each fry, one by one, dipping the ends of them into the puddle. He sipped and ate and tried to go back over the events.

How had they figured out her identity so soon? That was what bugged him the most. Plus, he'd thought that the body would go a lot farther down the river than it did, at least out of the city. He'd pictured some small-town sheriff finding her, some Barney Fife who wouldn't know jack shit about identifying bodies. But, instead, the city had it and was already linking her to the daycare center. He looked over at the people crowded around the bar laughing and joking with one another. He saw a pushing match start and worried for a moment about having to fight his way through a brawl to get to the door. But it dissolved into laughter before any real heat developed, and he leaned back in his chair. He had to get a grip.

Just then, the television channels flipped, and a *Breaking News* banner began to scroll along the bottom. First, there was Mia's face, the photograph taken in front of the daycare center. Then the baby's face flashed on the screen, and Julius choked, coughing out the liquid that had taken the wrong route down his throat. Jesus, he had to get out of there. He threw fifty bucks on the table and pushed out of his chair, catching it just before it tipped over. He could feel every bit of the alcohol in his system and teetered for a moment before forcing himself to stand still and upright. Then, with measured steps, he made his way out the door and into the evening. It was later than he'd thought, the light nearly gone from the sky as he made his way through the parking lot. He was standing next to it before he even recognized the car he'd been driving, and it took three tries before he managed to unlock the door and throw himself into the driver's seat. Fuck, there was no way he could drive.

He sat there, the harsh lights of the parking lot casting glare and shadows all around him and wondered what in the hell he would do next.

Tuesday afternoon, Audrey was relieved to see her dad standing in the hallway outside the counselor's doorway. She had spent more than an hour on the phone that morning, first with her mother and then with Sandy, as all of them mourned and speculated about Mia's death. Unfortunately, there were details that Audrey was not allowed to share, which had made navigating both conversations that much more difficult. Everyone wanted to know what it meant about Rosey, but no one had any answers, only heightened worries and more tears.

"Hi, Dad, I know this shouldn't feel like a relief, but . . ."

He pulled her into a quick hug before stepping back, holding both of her hands in his. "I know. I overheard a lot of the conversation with Mom this morning. I'm sorry you seem to be stuck in the middle of all of this."

"I just wish there was something I could do to help." She gestured at the door ahead of them. "And now this. It's a change of pace but, definitely not what I want to be thinking about."

He released her hands and knocked. "You can do this, kiddo. I know you can."

The meeting took more than an hour as the older woman took Audrey and her father through the steps that the trial would follow and the role she would be expected to play in it. Afterward, Audrey's father insisted on taking them both to dinner. Pittsburgh offered a wide variety of Italian restaurants, but there was no question about where to go. The small, family-owned pizza parlor had been there since Audrey was a child, and on a day like this, she was craving the familiar. They ordered two salads and a pizza to share. "It helps knowing what to expect tomorrow, don't you think?" He covered the end of a breadstick in soft butter and used it to gesture with before popping the end of it into his mouth.

"It does. I've sat in on parts of a few trials before, but I've never paid attention to the different stages that they go through. It still surprises me that both sides know so much about each other's plans before it ever starts. I think maybe it's good that Gabriel hasn't told me any more about what Adams's lawyer is planning. I'm nervous enough as it is."

"I think I'm a little bit afraid to hear all the exact details myself. Have you told us everything? Will there be surprises tomorrow?"

Audrey paused, resting her breadstick on the side of the salad bowl. As she lowered her gaze for a moment, it all seemed to come flooding back, the pain, the terror, and worst of all, the fear that she would be too late, and her parents killed because of it. She raised her eyes then and looked into the worried face of her father. "You know the story, Dad. It was just. I don't know." She let out a breath. "It was more than I said. More painful, more frightening." Her hands shook slightly, and she folded them together in her lap. "Back when I was little and found Toby's body, I had to tell my story so many times, to you and Mom, to the police, to the judge. And this was the same way, over and over, I had to tell what happened. Finally, I needed to give myself a little distance from it, not go into the depths of how I felt. Now, having to tell it again in all its detail, in front of a jury that may or may not believe me, it scares me to death."

"You know, Audrey, I think what impresses me the most is how you've survived all of that and managed to move forward with your life. Your mother and I never thought you'd be able to continue working for the police. We thought it would be too hard for you. But we were wrong. You have a solid core, honey, a sense of who you are and how you should be in the world, and at least so far, you haven't let Gary Adams take that away from you. I think, if you keep that in mind tomorrow and through the length of the trial, you're going to be okay."

Audrey looked up as the waitress delivered their pizza, grateful for the distraction. She squeezed her father's hand and then dug in her purse for a tissue. She refused to give in to tears, wouldn't let Adams have that even now. Instead, she dabbed at her eyes and then grinned across the table at her dad. "Thank you, Dad. It means a lot to me to hear you say that and to know that you're going to be sitting next to me. For now, though, let's have pizza and small talk, no big discussions or worries."

"Sounds good to me, honey. Tell me about the next wedding you've got coming up."

Audrey grinned, happy to comply.

Wednesday morning, Audrey was up before six, her stomach churning in anticipation of the trial beginning. She made herself some coffee but could only get through half a cup before setting it aside. She managed a few bites of bread and part of a banana but then gave up altogether and went to get dressed. Gabriel hadn't had much advice about what to wear, so she selected a simple blue skirt and a short-sleeved, white blouse. She put on some small hoop earrings and left it at that. Her face looked so pale in the bathroom mirror that she took a few extra minutes with her makeup. But even with all of that, she was ready a full hour before time to leave.

When her phone buzzed in her pocket, she was surprised to see that Rod was on his way up. Once inside, he simply opened his arms, and she fell into his embrace. Both of them held on tight for a few minutes before stepping back for a kiss. "Thank you so much. I needed that!" Audrey spoke as she and Rod sat down together on the sofa.

"I figured the nerves might be getting to you. How are you doing?"

"I'm okay."

"Nuh-uh, not the pro forma answer, the real one. How are you doing?"

"For real? I'm scared shitless, of the trial, of seeing Adams, of saying the wrong thing, of not being believed."

"You're perfectly normal then, is that what you're telling me?"

Audrey couldn't help but laugh. "Does all of that make me normal, not some hot mess that's going to dissolve on the stand?"

"Normal, plain normal, and you are not going to dissolve. Listen," he folded both of her hands in his. "I was there that day. I saw you right after you got away from him and all I wanted to do was get you to a hospital. You were so beat up." He shook his head. "But you wouldn't let me. In the midst of all that pain, your only thought was to protect your parents, to get to them before Adams could. I know what sort of toughness you've got inside of you, Audrey, and it's going to shine through today. I just wish I could be inside the courtroom to see it."

"Thank you, Rod. Between you and my dad, I almost believe it. Do you know when you'll have to testify? Has Gabriel said anything to you?"

"He's not sure. He doesn't think the opening statements will take very long at all, so it may be sometime today. I'm going to head to the precinct until I get a call. Then I'll be over."

"No more word about Mia Novak, I take it?"

"Smitty's been all over her records, but there's not a whole lot to find. Her roommate is in shock. He's been talking with her as well as the cousin and others at the bar, but they don't have much information on the boyfriend still."

"Nothing in the receipts?"

"Nah, looks like he's a cash guy." Rod ticked the items off on his hand. "It could mean he's careful about what he spends, or maybe he's married and doesn't want the wife to know where he's been, or maybe he's just less comfortable with cards. It's hard to know. We're working on it, but it's a pretty unproductive slog at this point, I'm sorry to say."

An alarm on Audrey's laptop began to flash then, and she stood to turn it off. "Time to get going, I guess." Her phone buzzed as well, and she saw her dad's text 'out front'.

Rod walked her out and held her again before she stepped away and climbed into her dad's car. Her eyes lingered on Rod as they pulled away from the curb before she turned her attention to her father. "Thanks for picking me up, Dad. It felt like it'd be pretty weird to Uber to a court trial."

Her dad laughed and kept up a steady patter of small talk as they covered the distance and then parked. As they walked down the wide city sidewalk to the courthouse, Audrey remembered long ago when she'd been taken to see the judge during Adams's trial for killing his son. Then, she'd held on to both of her parents' hands, and they'd lifted her up and over the wide metal grates. Even now, she found herself stepping around them, still not liking the sense of darkness and uncertainty that lurked beneath them. Then, she caught her father's eye.

"Some things never change, do they, Audie? I can remember your mom and me jumping you over them when you were a little girl."

The imposing courthouse appeared in front of them then, its massive granite blocks creating a look more like a castle than a municipal building. Construction was blocking the area around the courtyard fountain, and they could see a gaggle of press gathering near the front, so they entered through the side of the building. Since she'd begun working for the police department, the place had become more familiar to Audrey, but she realized that a part of her still felt like that frightened little girl who'd come to tell the judge about finding her friend's body. Audrey took her father's hand, glad that he was with her once again.

Sandy sat on the sofa with another pile of baby laundry, folding green outfit after green outfit, then pausing as a single purple one emerged from the stack. She held it up to her nose, but only the scent of detergent greeted her, nothing that hinted it was Rosey's. She tossed it aside and picked up the remote, turning quickly to the local news channel. Her mother and Audrey's mother came into the living room at the sound, Brigette Markum carrying a wooden tray with coffee and a platter of sweet rolls. She set it on the coffee table where Sandy and her mother could both reach it as the three of them settled close together on the sofa.

"*First day of the trial for Gary Adams in the attempted murder of Ms. Audrey Markum and the aggravated assault of two officers from the . . .*" Sandy hit the mute button, and they watched as a montage of still photographs filled the screen.

"Do you think they're inside already?" Sandy asked Brigette.

"I had a text from Mitch about ten minutes ago. He said they managed to get in before the press caught up with them."

"That's good," offered Cecelia. "Brigette, are you sure you wouldn't rather be there with them?"

Brigette reached for one of the small plates and a roll, balancing them in her lap. "It's okay. I know Audrey's glad that her dad is there sitting next to her." She sounded calm, Sandy thought, but she could see the tremor in her hand. "They'll keep me posted."

"What happens first?" Sandy set the laundry aside and leaned back with a cup of the fresh coffee. She'd lost track of how many cups she'd already had that day and worried for a moment before dismissing the concern and focusing back on the television.

"Mitch said that the counselor and the lawyer took Audrey through the steps. The jury was already set, so this morning there will be opening statements followed by the prosecution calling its witnesses."

"And will Audrey have to testify?" Cecelia asked as she shifted her weight from one hip to the other. Sandy thought her mother would have been better off in the armchair, but for some reason that morning, they seemed to want to huddle close to each other.

Brigitte nodded. "Yes, she's not first on the list, but she had no choice but to tell her story."

"I would be such a wreck." Sandy set her cup down and resumed folding the mound of baby clothes. She turned the sound back on as the piece on the trial wrapped up. Then, the photograph of Mia Novak appeared on the screen once again, this time in a split image with one of Rosey's baby pictures. The three women just stared, breakfast forgotten in the rush of feelings that accompanied the new report. Once it finished, Sandy snapped off the set. "I can't understand Mia's role in all of this. She was such a sweet girl, always so helpful. And now she's dead? Brigette, has Audrey said anything more about what they know?"

"No, not that I've heard. But, hon, she may not be allowed to tell us everything that she knows. I hate to say it, but she was there taking the photographs when they brought the body out of the river."

"My God," Cecelia looked horrified. "How can she do that kind of work, especially when her wedding photographs are so beautiful?"

"I don't know how she does it either," Brigette added, "but it does pay the bills."

"And it's how she met Rod." Sandy loaded the clothes into the basket and set it beside them on the floor. "It's so unreal that we've all ended up in these horrible situations at the same time. It's too much." She pulled a crumpled tissue from her pocket and dabbed at her eyes before blowing her nose and shoving the tissue back into her sweatshirt pocket.

"It's not too much," Cecelia leaned over and patted her daughter on the knee. "We're getting through it. Soon Adams will be back in jail where he belongs, and Rosey will be back home with us. I can feel it."

Sandy caught hold of her mother's hand and held on to it. "How do you stay so positive, Mom? I feel like I'm going to shatter into a million pieces."

"I just believe that as women, we're stronger than we think. And when we're together like this, helping each other, we're stronger still. You'll get through this. I know it. We all will."

Sandy watched as Brigette leaned over to take her mother's other hand, and the three of them held on, no longer talking but feeling the strength flow through them one to another.

As Audrey and her father made their way down the hall to the court-room, she was surprised to see the number of people gathered outside the double doors. It felt as if all of them were staring at her, covering their mouths, and raising their eyebrows as she passed She felt sick to her stomach and was glad that she hadn't been able to eat any more breakfast. Near the door, she spotted her lawyer, Gabriel. He waved her over and held out his hand. "How are you holding up, Audrey?"

She took his hand and noticed that he shook it and then held on a moment longer than usual. "I'm okay, I guess. I don't think you've met my dad. Gabriel Perez, this is Mitch Markum. The counselor told me that he could sit with me."

Gabriel released Audrey's hand and reached toward her father. "Mr. Markum, welcome. I'm glad Audrey has someone in her corner with her."

"It's just Mitch. Good to meet you, too. You're going to take care of my girl, right?"

Gabriel grinned. "That's my intention. Getting her justice for what she went through is my only goal."

The doors opened then, with Gabriel and his assistant admitted first. Audrey and her father followed in their wake, taking seats in the row just behind the prosecutor's table. She could hear the small crowd fol-lowing in after them, but she kept her gaze focused straight ahead. After a few minutes, a pert, young woman in an ill-fitting blue suit settled at the table next to Gabriel and began pulling a series of file folders out of a backpack. There was a stir in the crowd, and then Gary Adams walked into the courtroom between two armed guards and sat down at the woman's table. Audrey wished he'd been handcuffed and clad in prison orange, but instead, he was dressed neatly in a collared shirt and black slacks. He'd even had a haircut. He looked like an ordinary man, she thought, and turned her head away quickly, determined not to make eye contact. They all stood as the judge entered, and then everyone was seated once again.

Audrey remembered the woman judge she'd met when she came to the courthouse as a child, but this judge had none of the warmth and caring that had stuck in Audrey's memory. This man looked to be a little younger than her father. He had close-cropped brown hair and thin, rimless eyeglasses. As he sat down, Audrey thought he seemed almost giddy with excitement as though he was thrilled to be a part of the spectacle that the case was becoming. It did not seem like a good sign, and Audrey looked over at Gabriel to assess his reaction. But Gabriel was already focused on his notes, perhaps a little nervous himself, as he would be the first to speak. She looked at her father then, and once again, he took her hand in his and rested them both on his knee. Then, Gabriel stood to speak.

It's not like on TV, Audrey thought, as she watched him stand and walk to the small podium that stood between the two tables. She knew from other trials that there was never the pacing or walking around that television liked to use to add suspense and excitement to the show. Instead, trials were entirely controlled with one individual and then the other standing and talking into the fixed microphone.

The judge nodded for him to begin. Audrey liked Gabriel's voice and thought that he sounded calm and confident, despite any nerves that he might be experiencing. "Ladies and gentlemen, thank you for being here today. My statement this morning is going to be simple and brief. The facts, in this case, are overwhelmingly clear, and there is no need to take more of your time than is necessary. Gary Adams, whom you see here, has been accused of two crimes, the attempted murder of Ms. Audrey Markum and the aggravated assault on two police officers. We will demonstrate how Mr. Adams took meticulous steps to stalk and then capture my client before beating her and leaving her for dead. We will show that he then rented a car, bought himself some breakfast, and drove to Ms. Markum's parents' home in order to kill them as well. The police officers that he shot at merely got in his way. We are fortunate that neither of them were killed. To be clear, there was nothing random about this assault on Audrey Markum. The attack was premeditated, which is why attempted murder in the first degree is the key charge here today. Let me be blunt. When Mr. Adams left Ms. Markum beaten and broken, tossed unconscious on the floor of an apartment he had rented solely for the purpose of attacking her, he believed he had completed his task and that she was dead." Audrey watched Gabriel speak, wondering what others in the room thought as he made his points. "It is solely because of Ms. Markum's indomitable strength of spirit and determined self-preservation that she is sitting here with us today. Now, she needs your help and strength to receive the justice that is due her following such a despicable attack."

Audrey looked at Gabriel and then at the jurors, but she could read very little on anyone's face. Then it was Gary Adams's lawyer's turn to speak, and Audrey found herself holding her breath. Audrey thought that the small woman looked more nervous than Gabriel had as she settled her notes in front of her on the podium and cleared her throat before beginning. "Your Honor, ladies and gentlemen of the jury. As you all know, the charge of first-degree attempted murder is a very serious one and requires, most importantly, that the state prove that a crime was planned ahead of time, that it was premeditated. Although the prosecution has cobbled together a set of coincidences and circumstantial evidence, I am confident that you will easily see through it. There are no witnesses to the alleged attack or to any planning ahead of time. Instead, there is just Ms. Markum's word, the word of a woman sitting here today, clearly unscathed, in good health, and no doubt basking in the attention. Thank you."

With that, the attorney sat and, as Audrey let out the breath she'd been holding, she felt her shoulders sinking with fear and disappointment. It was going to be so much more difficult than she had ever imagined it would be.

"Mr. Perez, are you ready to call your first witness?"

"Yes, Your Honor, I am. I'd like to call Mr. Sunan Dhaliwal." Audrey watched as Sunan made his way carefully to the witness chair and was sworn in. Then, Gabriel began his questioning. "Mr. Dhaliwal, could you please tell us your occupation and where you work?"

"Yes," Sunan began, and Audrey worried that he looked even more anxious than he did in the market when his mother-in-law was looking over his shoulder. A bead of sweat had formed on his upper lip, and he reached to wipe it off before returning his hands to his lap. "I work in a food store, The Corner Market, it is called. I manage the checkout and the ordering of items for the store."

"Do you own the market, Mr. Dhaliwal?"

"No sir, I manage it for my mother-in-law."

"How many days a week do you work there?"

Audrey thought Sunan looked a little puzzled by the question. "I work whenever the market is open. We are only closed for the major holidays."

"You are at the cash register every day?"

"Yes."

"And do you get to know many of your customers? Do you chat with any of them?"

"There is not a lot of time to chat but, yes, I do know many, many of our customers. I believe most of them live or work in the neighborhood. We are very convenient."

Audrey grinned at this and noticed Gabriel smiling slightly as well. "Are you familiar with Ms. Markum?"

"Oh yes, Ms. Audrey is in quite often. She is always friendly and asks about my new granddaughter."

"Thank you. Now, have you ever seen Mr. Adams in your store, the defendant here today?"

The smile dropped from Sunan's face as he answered this question. The nervousness suddenly returned. "Yes, I recognize him from the store."

"Did he shop there often?"

"No, no, only once."

"But you remember him after only meeting him once? Why is that?"

"It was the Wednesday before Ms. Audrey was attacked. Mr. Adams introduced himself to me and told me that he was Ms. Audrey's friend."

"And did you believe him?"

"Objection!" Adams's lawyer interjected. "Irrelevant."

"I withdraw the question, Your Honor." Gabriel looked again at Sunan. "Thank you, Mr. Dhaliwal. That is all."

Gabriel sat, and Adams's lawyer stepped up to the microphone once again. "Mr. Dhaliwal, can you tell us what Mr. Adams said when he was in your store?"

"Yes, he said that he was a friend of Ms. Audrey, and he asked me to tell her he said hello."

"Did he ask for any details about her, where she lived, or when she shopped?"

"No, ma'am."

"Did he threaten her in any way during your conversation?"

"No, ma'am. He did not."

"He said to tell her hi." She repeated and looked up at the judge. "No further questions, your honor."

Sunan was dismissed and sat down several rows behind Audrey as Gabriel stood at the podium once more. "I'd like to call Mrs. Ishani Patel, please."

Mrs. Patel was dressed in one of her most beautiful saris, the deep reds blazing as she walked to the witness stand and sat down carefully. Once she was sworn in, Gabriel began again. "Mrs. Patel, we appreciate your coming in today." Mrs. Patel nodded but said nothing, and Audrey thought that she heard a small laugh from Adams. "Are you the owner of the market where Mr. Dhaliwal is employed?"

Audrey admired how Mrs. Patel sat with an almost regal posture, her age not dimming her strength in any apparent way. "Yes, my late husband and I bought The Corner Market more than forty years ago."

"And is it open nearly every day as Mr. Dhaliwal said?"

"Yes, every day except today."

Gabriel seemed surprised. "You closed the store today? I thought you only closed on the major holidays."

"This was too important. I would have asked my daughter to run it today, but she is home watching the baby."

"Mrs. Patel, do you know Ms. Audrey Markum?" Audrey was shocked at the warmth of the woman's smile as she answered.

"Yes, Ms. Audrey is a regular customer. She does not cook very often and does not plan her meals ahead of time. She comes to the store two or three times every week." She spoke with her beautiful, crisp accent, and Audrey watched as Adams seemed to squirm for a moment.

She wanted to blush with embarrassment, but Mrs. Patel's gaze was steady and reassuring, so she accepted the judgment of her cooking routines and waited for Gabriel to ask his next question. "Mrs. Patel, have you ever seen the defendant in your store?"

"Yes, I saw him at the same time my son-in-law did. I didn't like him."

"You didn't like Mr. Adams? Why is that?"

"He was not real, not genuine in what he said. I could tell that he was not Ms. Audrey's friend."

Adam's attorney stood quickly. "Objection, your honor."

The judge nodded. "Overruled. I'd urge caution, though, Mr. Perez."

"Yes, sir. Mrs. Patel, why do you say that Mr. Adams was not her friend?"

"Pshh, after forty years in a market, I know how to read people. He bought two bananas and a can of soup. He was pretending."

The attorney popped up again. "Objection."

"Sustained, Mr. Perez. Let's move on."

"Mrs. Patel, can you please tell us about the following day? What happened the next morning when Ms. Markum came into the market, and Mr. Dhaliwal delivered the message from Mr. Adams?"

"It was clear to me that she was shocked and afraid. I asked Sunan to walk her home."

"And did he?"

She shook her head. "No, Ms. Audrey would not accept his help."

"You were worried for her safety, Mrs. Patel?"

"Yes, I was."

"Thank you. No more questions."

Adams's lawyer returned to the podium. "Mrs. Patel, how many people shop in your store in a single week?"

Mrs. Patel sat even straighter. "We are very prosperous. We have over 2000 transactions every week."

"And does one transaction mean one customer?"

"No, sometimes people come in together."

"Then you must see hundreds and hundreds of customers each week. Is this what you're saying?"

"Yes."

"And how many of those customers do you know?"

Audrey saw Mrs. Patel's shoulders stiffen as she paused to consider the question. A single cough sounded from the back of the room, but the silence returned. Finally, Mrs. Patel looked down at her lap and then up into the face of the questioner. "I believe I recognize most of them. We are a neighborhood market."

"You say that you recognize most of them. Out of the hundreds of shoppers each week, how many do you know by name?"

Audrey saw Gabriel's pen bounce between his fingers as they waited. "I believe I know more than three hundred by name. Many people like Ms. Audrey shop several times a week."

"I'm sorry, Mrs. Patel, but you see scores and scores of customers a week, and you expect us to believe that you remember a single interaction with a single man?" The lawyer made a dismissive sound as she waved her hand. "No more questions, your honor."

Audrey looked to see if Gabriel would question her further, but with a slight shake of his head, he responded, "No redirect, your honor."

Mrs. Patel stood and arranged her sari carefully before stepping down and walking back toward her seat. She made a quick gesture, and Sunan stood, the two of them making their way to the back of the room. They walked out proudly, their eyes looking straight ahead, but Audrey thought that their shoulders had a sag to them that she hadn't seen before. She hoped they'd open the store once they got back.

Rod walked in and was happy to see Smitty looking at home back at his old desk in the homicide division. Rod shoved his partner's ball cap forward before sitting down across from him at his own desk. There was no point in asking yet again how the man was doing. He was there, he was obviously tired, but he was working the case. Healing takes time, Rod thought, as his brain skittered back to the spring when he'd nearly lost both Smitty and Audrey. He forced himself to push all of that aside. "All right, what have we got?"

Smitty settled the cap back into place without skipping a beat. "We're still waiting on the full report from the M.E., but the preliminary information puts time of death less than a week ago."

"So, Thursday night, she meets up with her boyfriend at the bar, takes him out back through the kitchen, and no one sees her again. That's within our time frame."

"Yep." He turned back to his computer screen as an alert dinged. "Okay, here it is." Smitty angled the screen and hit a few keys, and Rod was looking at the medical examiner's report as well.

They read silently for a minute or two before both of them looked up. "It fits."

"Yep." Smitty read from the report. "Cause of death: traumatic brain injury, rating severe with intracranial bleeding stemming from a triangular-shaped contusion on the back of the skull."

Rod continued reading. "Blood type, contusion shape and depth are consistent with the crime scene report which identifies the corner of the concrete slab where the blood pool was heaviest."

Smitty leaned back in his chair as he tapped his thumb against the armrest. "Okay, what do we know?"

"I'm not sure that we know anything for sure. I'm fairly convinced that Mia took the baby. She could have bundled her up in the bed linens that were mentioned or some other laundry. I think she runs down that back hallway and puts the bundle somewhere before opening the back door. After that, she dashes back out front to join the others at the fire drill. Meanwhile, whoever she was taking the baby for, picks up the bundle and takes off."

"But we still don't know who that was. Do we think they murdered Mia?"

Rod shrugged. "I don't know. They could have. Maybe they didn't think she'd stand up to police questioning. Who knows? The situation definitely went pear-shaped when she hit her head on the concrete, though. I don't see how a dead accomplice would have done the baby stealer any good. Seems like it'd just add heat to the situation."

"Makes sense. We still only have bits and pieces of the car from the traffic cams, sedan, dark, older with very little chrome left on it."

"No plate, though, right?"

"Just one number and that was blurry. It could be anywhere in the city by now."

"So, he takes the baby somewhere and leaves it, right? Sells it, maybe? Because he didn't have a baby with him at the bar that night."

"That's right. Shit, we may never find this baby, especially if the accomplice sold it." He looked over at Rod. "This is going to kill your friends if we can't find her, isn't it?"

"It's going to be damned hard to accept. I know that much. Even a bad answer can be easier to handle than an unanswered one. Not knowing, that's the real killer."

"Our first question is, where did he put the baby before he went to the bar? Then, after he meets up with Mia and dumps her body in the river, where did he go after that? Is he done with the baby or not?"

"Did the busboy at the bar sit down with the sketch artist?"

"He did, but the artist said he didn't get much, thought the kid was guessing more than remembering. "

"Average white guy, that's all we've got, right? Roughly five-ten, brown hair, maybe brown eyes, average build. It's not much."

"Mia's roommate didn't have any more information on the guy?"

"No, she said she only saw him once, and that was just briefly one evening when she was heading out. Did you finish putting together the warrant for her apartment?"

Smitty stood, pushed his chair back, and stretched his arms overhead. "Yeah. That's where I'm headed now. Once I've got it, I'll get the team over there, but you know it's not fast. Even if they find DNA from someone, it may take weeks to process, and if they're not in the system . . ." He raised his hands in a gesture of futility. "Are you headed over to the courthouse soon?"

"I'm not sure. The attorney texted me saying he thinks I might be up mid-afternoon, but it could be later, tomorrow even."

"How's Audrey holding up, do you know?"

Rod began collecting items from his desk. "I don't know. She was a little shaky this morning. I hate that I can't be there."

Smitty rested his hand on Rod's shoulder. "She's a tough cookie if you ask me. She'll be all right. Talk to you later."

"Yep, see ya." Rod turned back to his computer, thinking of what little they knew about the case. 'Jewels'. What could that be a nickname for? Julien? Jude? Julius? And all of that presumed that he had an English-sounding name, that it didn't stand for initials or something else altogether. That wasn't going to get him anywhere if he didn't find out something more about the car.

Rod dug in his bag and pulled out a squashed granola bar. He peeled the wrapper off, catching the loose bits as it started to crumble. As he chewed, he thought about the journey that Mia's body had made. With an enlarged city map on the screen, he followed the line of the river back upstream from where she'd been found. The Allegheny branch came in from the northeast along one of the busier parts of the city with the sports stadiums and more touristy areas. He searched along a good stretch of it, but most of it seemed like an unlikely dumping site. On the other hand, the Monongahela had a more private, industrial feel to it. Barges came through regularly, and there were some older, industrial sites along its southern bank. If he were looking for a spot to dump it, that was a more likely area. Rod had a rough time frame in mind, so he dropped the empty wrapper in the trash and headed down the hall to talk with one of their technicians about street cameras.

35

Hannah Dudnyk held little Joy against her chest as she turned the heat off on the oven. Julius's dinner would be dried out and inedible if he didn't get home soon. She was a little surprised not to have gotten a call from him, but his work often kept him late and didn't offer an opportunity to phone home. Or at least, that's what he said. Hannah had worked for the same company years ago and sometimes struggled to match her husband's description of the job with her recollections.

While Joy was sleeping that afternoon, Hannah had brought up the fat box from the basement and set to work assembling the baby swing she'd bought months ago. The directions didn't consist of much more than a detailed diagram, but that was all she needed. It required only a few tools and came together quickly. Once she'd inserted batteries into the swing's music box, she set it up in the kitchen near the window and tested it out. Perfect. There were three different speeds for it as well as a small variety of tunes, and she just knew that Joy would love it. Perhaps it would even help with the colic. Hannah didn't mind the crying, but she knew it bothered Julius. She wanted him to love the baby as much as she did, and she worried that Joy's constant crying was making that difficult.

Before her own dinner got any colder, Hannah went up and changed Joy and brought her downstairs. She settled her in the new swing and started it rocking. Then, she got her plate and silverware and set them at the place next to the swing. Once she'd served her plate, she pushed the button on the small TV so that she could check on the news while she ate. The button didn't seem to work, though, so she located the little-used remote and tried that. Nothing. She shifted her plate on the table before pulling the TV out away from the wall. The cord was dangling down, unplugged from the socket. How had that happened, she wondered as she fastened it back in? The set turned on immediately, and she turned the volume down so that it wouldn't disturb Joy.

With the sound off, she could still make out most of the stories, given the graphics and other news scrolling across the bottom. There was a photograph of a local businessman whose name she knew from her tax work. It looked as though he was starting a run for some sort of state office. As she ate, she wondered how long it would be until some sharp reporter started looking into his finances. Once they got a look at some of the businesses he was involved with, more than a few eyebrows would be raised. Oh well, no skin off her nose. All she'd done were his taxes. The anchor reappeared then, beside a photograph of a young woman. Curious, Hannah was just about to turn up the volume when Joy let out a piercing shriek. She turned away from the set and began unbuckling the baby. She lifted her out carefully and held her close, the cries subsiding as she rested her cheek on the top of the baby's head. When Hannah turned back to face the TV, two photographs were side by side on the screen, one of the young woman and another of an infant. Hannah blinked, and the images dissolved into an ad for dishwasher detergent.

Hannah stood for a moment in the center of the kitchen, swaying with the baby in her arms. A slight breeze blew in through the window, and she caught the scent of fading roses and newly cut grass. She took the bottle that she'd prepared before dinner and tested the temperature on her wrist the way she remembered seeing her mother do it for her baby brother's bottles. It was now the perfect temperature. She held it in her left hand as she reached behind the television and unplugged it once again. "Let's go upstairs to your room for your bottle, sweetie."

As Sunan and his mother-in-law left the courtroom, Gabriel Perez returned to the podium. "Your honor, I'd like to call Mr. Justin Inouye to the stand." A young man that Audrey had never seen before walked quickly up the center aisle and took his seat. He was wearing a dark green polo shirt, and his thick black hair was piled artfully to one side of his head. He was sworn in quickly, and Gabriel began his questions. "Mr. Inouye, have you ever met the defendant, Mr. Adams, sitting here today?"

"No, no, I haven't, not in person."

"Have you met him in some other fashion?" Gabriel tilted his head to the side slightly.

"The police told me that he's the person who sublet my apartment in the spring."

"But if you never met him, how did you arrange the sublet?"

"I had put up a card in the coffee shop."

"Is this the coffee shop right near your building?"

"Yes."

"And did you advertise it anywhere else? Post it online somewhere maybe?"

"No, I like to get someone local when I can. I didn't want to have to pay an agency or anything, so this just seemed simpler."

"All right, go ahead."

"So, I got an email asking me about renting it. We traded a couple of emails, and once I had the money, I left a key for him with a neighbor."

He paused before adding, "But Adams isn't the name he gave me. I was told that later."

"I understand." Gabriel nodded patiently. "Did he have references? Did you look into him at all before leasing your apartment to him?"

The young man looked offended, his self-assurance slipping a bit. "Sure, I got a reference letter from him. It was just gonna be for a month anyway."

"And did you call the reference? Speak to anyone about Mr. Adams before arranging for him to rent your apartment?"

The young man leaned back and shook his head. "No."

"Now, you had been gone just over a week when the police called you, is that correct?"

"Yes, I was in Atlanta for work. When they told me what happened, I flew home."

"And what happened then?"

"When I got to my apartment, there was police tape across the front door, and I had to call for a police officer to come and let me in."

"And what did you find once you went inside?"

He lifted his hands and spread them wide. "There was nothing. It looked normal to me. I couldn't see what the fuss was all about."

"And did the police tell you why they'd called you home?"

"They said someone had been tortured in my apartment."

Adams's lawyer jumped to her feet. "Objection, your honor. Calls for hearsay."

"Withdrawn," Gabriel answered quickly. "No further questions."

As he sat back down, Audrey looked again at the jury, and they seemed genuinely puzzled by the sequence, but she closed her eyes and could picture the apartment, the widescreen TV, the black leather couch, the cords biting into her wrists and ankles as she twisted to try and get free. Without realizing it, she gripped her father's hand tightly. He held on to her and placed his other hand on top of hers. Then, Adams's attorney took Gabriel's place at the podium.

"Mr. Inouye, have you ever sublet your apartment before?"

"Sure, lots of times."

"And do you generally do a deep background check on people who offer to sublet from you?"

"Nah, I usually find someone from the neighborhood, and it's never for very long. Besides, I keep anything valuable with me. I just don't like leaving it empty when I have to be away."

"And have there ever been any issues with sub-letters in the past?"

"Just one. Some asshole brought his dogs with him, and when they left, the place was full of fleas."

"I'm sure that must have been very frustrating. No more questions, your honor."

The judge banged the gavel once and then spoke. "We'll have a lunch recess now. I'd like everyone back in their places by 1:30 sharp." A hum started to fill the room as everyone stood. Audrey watched the two guards come and take Adams back out the door he'd come in, but she turned away quickly when Adams looked her way. Gabriel twisted around to talk with Audrey and her father.

"How are you two holding up?" He spoke as he stacked his notes and slid them into a slim briefcase.

Audrey was still holding on to her dad's hand, but he didn't seem to mind. "We're okay."

Gabriel paused and rested his hand on Audrey's shoulder. "Are you going to be ready to tell your story this afternoon?"

Audrey took a deep breath before answering. "I think I'd just as soon get it over with, so yeah. I'll be ready."

"All right then, see you back here." He gestured behind him toward a door. "If you go out that way, you should be able to avoid the press."

Audrey's dad shook Gabriel's hand and then walked with her toward the door. Audrey was starving but wasn't at all sure whether she'd be able to eat anything. When they emerged from the courtroom, they found themselves next to a back stairway that led down to the street. Audrey's father stuck his head out the door first, but there were no reporters on their side of the building. "Coast is clear," he announced, and Audrey followed him out. Two blocks down, they found a sandwich shop. They ordered a single chicken salad sub and had the server cut it in half for them. Audrey knew she couldn't keep much more than that down at this point. They tried to make small talk as they ate, but eventually, silence won out, and they sat together quietly, watching the people passing by outside the shop.

Before going back into the courtroom, Audrey stopped in the restroom and took a few minutes to wash her face. The cool water felt good, and she took her time before drying her face with the coarse paper towels. She touched up the little bit of makeup she'd been wearing and then squared her shoulders. She was grateful to have the bathroom to herself as she took an extra minute to look herself in the eye and whisper, "you can do this." Then, she went to rejoin her father. Adams was brought in, and everything started up once again.

Gabriel moved to the podium. "Your honor, the prosecution calls Ms. Audrey Markum." Audrey's father squeezed her hand once more before she stood and walked to the witness chair. Her hands were shaking, so she tucked them under her legs as soon as she'd been sworn in. When she looked up at Gabriel, he gave her a quick wink and then spoke. "Ms. Markum, what we'd like to hear this afternoon is your account of what happened to you this spring. Can you begin by telling the jury what line of work you're in?"

Audrey held her head up as she spoke. "I have my own wedding photography business. I also work as a photographer for the Pittsburgh police department."

"Thank you. Now you work primarily from your home, is that correct?"

"Yes."

"You live in an apartment building, is that right?"

"Yes, it is."

"Now, can you describe for us the events this spring? Please take your time and start at the very beginning."

"When the weather started to get warm, I was outside more than usual. Early that week, some simple things happened that just made me a little bit nervous. The light over the entrance to my apartment burned out, and when I was in my kitchen one evening, I thought I saw a man standing under a tree outside my building. I contacted my landlord about the light."

"And was it repaired?"

Audrey shook her head. "No, not right away."

"Then what happened?"

"On Wednesday morning, I was out with my camera taking pictures around my neighborhood. I thought I saw Mr. Adams at a table in a coffee shop near my home." Audrey gestured with her chin toward where Adams was sitting but did her best not to look the man in the eye.

"Is this the shop that Mr. Inouye mentioned? Does it have a bulletin board of sorts?"

Audrey nodded. "Yes, there are always notices for lost dogs or things like that."

"All right. So, you saw him. Did you get a photograph of him?"

"No, once I zoomed in, he had moved out of sight."

"That was Wednesday, you say. What happened next?"

"The next day, Thursday, I was at the market near my house picking up some groceries to make dinner that night. When I was checking out, Sunan and Mrs. Patel told me that Mr. Adams had been there and told them that he knew me."

"And how did that make you feel?"

"I was terrified. I hurried home and locked my door."

"Why did this frighten you, Ms. Markum?"

"It was a name that I thought I knew." She tried to answer carefully, knowing the rules that Gabriel had laid out.

"All right, then what did you do?"

"That evening, my boyfriend came over for dinner, and we talked about how I could protect myself. He suggested that I alter my regular routines and contact the landlord about updating the outside security system."

"Did you take both of those steps?"

"Yes," Audrey nodded. "The landlord said he would see to the system the following week. In the meantime, I arranged to be dropped off and picked up at my gym rather than walk there and back on my own."

"What happened the next day, on Friday, Ms. Markum?"

Audrey took a deep breath, pulled her hands from under her legs, and squeezed them tightly in her lap. "That night, I was photographing a rehearsal dinner at a hotel downtown. I didn't expect to be out late, but the groom's family insisted I stay for dinner and dancing afterward. Around ten-thirty, I called a ride service to take me home. The music had given me a splitting headache, so once I was in the car and the driver had the address, I took out my hearing aids and tucked them into my camera bag. When we arrived at my building, I entered the driver's tip before I got out of the car and then walked quickly up to my apartment. I was reaching to unlock my door when I was grabbed from behind."

"Can you identify for the court who it was that grabbed you?"

"Yes, it was Mr. Adams."

"The defendant. Thank you. What did you do then?"

"I dropped my weight into my hips and flipped him over my head onto the floor." Audrey thought she might have heard a titter from the back of the courtroom, but she continued. "My camera bag was still on my shoulder, though, and he was tangled in it. When he stood up, I tried to scream, and he hit me in the head with a gun. I think I passed out for a few seconds because I woke up on the floor. When I came to, he grabbed me up by the arm and pressed a gun into my back. Then he made me walk across the street to another apartment."

"Did anyone see you, Ms. Markum?"

Audrey shook her head, wishing again that the street had not been deserted that night. "No, I don't think so. I didn't see anyone."

"What happened when you got to the other apartment?"

"He had a key to an outer door and an inner door. When he opened the door into the apartment, I saw a heavy, wooden chair in the middle of the room. He threw me into it and tied me up to it. Then he punched me in the face, and I passed out again."

Audrey shifted in her seat, releasing her hands, and forced her fingers apart, flexing them to restore the blood flow. "I was out for some time. I don't know how long. When I came to, he was sitting on the couch with his back to me, watching the TV. Without my hearing aids, I could see the game, but I couldn't hear it. A commercial came on, and he got up and came over to me. He was yelling at me, and he hit me some more, knocking me out again." Audrey made the mistake of looking over at her father then, and she could see the pain in his face, the anger layered on top of it. She wiped a tear from her eye and straightened her spine, determined to continue. "When I came to the next time, it was dark. The TV was off, and Adams was not in the room. The chair I was in was facing the front window, and I could see my apartment across the street." Audrey paused for a moment, remembering how that glow of safety had both taunted and reassured her that night. "Then he came back and teased me about that and tried to get me to talk to him. When I wouldn't, he started choking me. He hit me again with his pistol and told me that if I made any noise, he would kill me and then my parents. Then he left the room again and went down the hall. While it was dark and quiet, I found a way to get my feet out of my shoes and out of the cords. I managed to pick up the chair and shuffled carefully over to where my bag was lying on the floor. I used my feet to get my phone out, and I hid it in the waistband of my pants. Then the light went on in a room down the hall, so I snuck back to where I'd been."

"I'm sorry to make you go through this, Ms. Markum, but I want to be sure that the jury understands the situation clearly. Can you tell us what sort of shape you were in physically at that point?"

"My head was throbbing, my nose was broken and blocked with blood so that I couldn't breathe through it. My lips were split and bleeding as well. My throat was also in pain from the choking."

"Your honor, at this time, I'd like to introduce into evidence the photographs that were taken of Ms. Markum following her ordeal along with the medical report. The jurors can read the list of injuries, but I'd like them to make particular note of the broken nose, the heavily bruised eye socket, and the split lip that Ms. Markum just described."

"Allowed," the judge responded. As Gabriel handed several sets of prints to the bailiff to share with the jury, a widescreen to the left of Audrey filled with a photograph of her battered face. She heard a quick intake of breath from several members of the jury as she turned her head away. She didn't need to see it to know what it looked like. She knew her father had seen her at the time, but for some reason, she hated that he had to see it all again. She just wished it could all be over.

Gabriel continued. "Ms. Markum, what happened next, after you had the phone in your possession?"

"Adams came back into the room and tried again to get me to talk. He wanted me to beg for my life. When I refused to speak, he choked me again. Then he kept taunting me as he started cleaning up the apartment."

"Cleaning up?"

"He had a container of antiseptic wipes, and he was cleaning all of the places that he'd touched. He had a duffle bag where he put his things as well as my camera bag. He told me when he was done, he was going to go and kill my parents. I started to scream. He stuffed two of the cleaning wipes into my mouth and then tied a bandana around my mouth to keep them in. I couldn't breathe through my nose, so I knew I was going to die. I passed out."

Gabriel paused as the noise level grew in the courtroom, and the judge banged his gavel. "Order, order now." Once it was quiet, the judge spoke again. "Please continue, Ms. Markum."

"I was surprised when I woke up again. I found myself on the floor and noticed that the bandana had come loose and my hands were no longer tied. I immediately used my phone to text my friend so that he could come and get me, and we could check on my parents. I didn't know how long I had been unconscious or what Adams might have done while I was out."

"Why didn't you call 911 Ms. Markum? Weren't you in an emergency?"

"I couldn't hear well enough to use the telephone. My friend is a police detective, so I texted him instead. I was able to walk across the street to my apartment, and he met me there. Officers were sent to my parents' house, and we followed in another police car."

"Thank you, Ms. Markum. I know this has been difficult." He looked up at the judge. "No further questions, your honor."

The judge banged his gavel down and waited for the room to quiet once again. "Ladies and gentlemen, we will recess at this time and resume tomorrow morning at eight-thirty. Cross-examination will begin then." Audrey sat in the witness chair waiting as the judge stepped out and the guards returned for Adams. Once he was well away, she stood and walked back to where her dad stood next to Gabriel.

"You were brilliant, Audrey. Good work." Gabriel said as he touched Audrey lightly on the shoulder. Audrey nodded to him but didn't know what to say. Once he'd stepped away, her father opened his arms, and she melted into him.

"My God, Audrey. I still can't believe you're alive after all of that. I had no idea."

Audrey held on for a few more minutes before stepping back and looking at his face. "I'm so sorry you had to hear all of that, Dad, all of those details."

"You and Detective Rodriguez kept a lot of that to yourselves, didn't you?"

He looped his arm around her shoulder as they headed to the back stairway. "We didn't want to worry you and Mom."

"Well, I was impressed with how you did today, Audie, really impressed."

"Tomorrow's going to be a lot tougher, though, isn't it?"

"Probably. Do you want to come home, spend the night with your mom and me? We can be back here early in the morning."

"That's sweet of you, Dad. I appreciate it. Will it hurt your feelings if I say no, that I just want to be in my own place tonight?"

"Not at all. I understand. Let's get some take-out and have dinner at your place before I head home."

"Thanks, Dad, for all of this."

"Audrey, if I could give you the world, I would. Take-out food is the least I can offer! Why don't you see if Rod is free to join us?" She was surprised to find that even after a tough day like today, her dad could still make her smile.

Rod was happy to get the invitation from Audrey's father to join them for dinner. It had been a tedious day with hours spent going through the video records of dozens of cameras around the city. There were few cameras near the bar, but given the timeframe, they had done their best, matching three cars with the scenario that they had in mind. By the end of the day, he and Smitty thought that they might have narrowed that down to the make and model of the car, but little more. None of the cameras had caught more than two numbers on the plate, and there were simply too many of those records to sort through.

He found a parking spot a block down from Audrey's place, got out, and walked the distance slowly, passing alongside the apartment building where she had been held before crossing the street. An image flashed into his brain of Audrey's face when he came running into her apartment that day, and it made him wonder how things had gone in court. When she opened the door, he pulled Audrey into a deep kiss, but a laughing, fake cough from the next room brought him around. "Hey, Mr. Markum!" Rod called over Audrey's shoulder.

"Come on in, Rod," Audrey spoke as she slipped her arm around his waist and walked with him into the living room. He stepped forward to shake her father's hand and then took a seat on the sofa. From the kitchen area, Audrey called out. "It's Chinese take-out. Do you want wine or beer to go with it?"

"Beer'd be fine. So come on, tell me how it went today. What happened?"

Audrey opened the beer bottle and brought it over to the sofa before taking a seat beside him. "We were just discussing that, but I don't know how to describe it. What would you say, Dad?"

Mr. Markum held his half-empty wine glass close to his chest as he spoke. "Audrey did great. She really did. Her attorney, Gabriel, did a good job, too." He took a deep breath then, and Rod watched as the man seemed to struggle to hold himself together. "I have to say. It was tough to hear the details, even now, with Audrey sitting right next to me. I wanted to jump over the table and take the bastard out, I can tell you."

Rod nodded. "I know the feeling, know it well." He turned to Audrey. "Are you done testifying then?"

"Unfortunately, not. When it starts in the morning, it'll be the other attorney's turn to cross-examine me. That's the part that scares me."

Rod looked at her and then across the room at Mr. Markum. "Do you have any idea what their strategy is?"

"Audrey and I think she's trying to discount the idea that it was premeditated. I think they're going to describe his stalking as just a string of coincidences, that it wasn't planned out ahead of time."

"Well, that's a load of bullshit." Rod set his bottle on the coffee table and leaned back, pulling Audrey's hand into his and resting them in his lap. "I don't think the jury is going to buy that."

"I don't either." Audrey's father stood and gestured toward the counter. "Should we eat now, Audie? I don't want to be too late getting back home tonight."

Audrey and Rod both stood. "Of course. Let's set it all out." She turned toward Rod. "Dad got a big variety, so hopefully, you'll find something you like." Once they were settled around the table, Audrey looked at Rod. "Can you tell us about your day? Is there any news at all?"

Rod wiped his mouth on the small paper napkin before taking a sip of beer. "I wish I could say we'd made progress today, but it doesn't feel like it, I'm afraid. We're trying to find some details about the car in hopes that it will lead us somewhere."

"And the young woman from the daycare center? Can you tell us anything about her?"

"We don't know much about her at all, just that it looks like she probably did die back behind the cousin's bar."

Audrey's dad looked at him sadly. "That's not much to go on, is it?"

"Nope, a friggin' needle in a haystack as far as the car goes." Rod could see how crestfallen both Audrey and her father were, and it made him feel even worse. The truth was, he and Smitty were so frustrated they were starting to snap at each other. They'd both been relieved to leave the station today. "But we'll be back at it bright and early tomorrow."

"We know you will, Rod. We're glad that you and Smitty have this case. We know you'll do your best." Audrey's father eased the conversation onto more stable terrain then as they finished their meal. Once they finished, Audrey stood up and hugged her father, and Rod shook his hand. "See you in the morning, Audie!" He tipped an imaginary hat and left.

Rod scooted his chair back and pulled Audrey's up next to it. "Okay, Scout, now how are you really doing?"

Audrey dropped into the chair and ran her hands through her short hair, leaving much of it standing on end. "It was awful. I just hated for my dad to have to hear all of that."

"I can imagine. But he seemed fine. He's tough and willing to do anything for you."

"I know. It just makes me sad."

"And the anxiety? How was that today?"

"It was all right. I didn't panic. I'm so scared about tomorrow, though. I wish I knew what to expect."

"You're going to be fine. I know it. To be honest, I get anxious in court, too, whenever I have to testify. It's normal to feel that way. All you have to do is tell the truth, *your* truth, because you were the one who went through it all, not the lawyers."

"Thanks, I get that. So, Mia Novak? Any news on her that you couldn't share with my dad?"

"I wish there was, actually. We really were just chasing car videos all day. My hunch is that she was dumped on the south side of the Monongahela, so we were trying to link cars between there and the bar, but it's a damned big stretch of river." He raised his hands in a helpless gesture.

"Poor little Rosey. I keep hoping that whoever took her wanted her. The idea of someone selling her just makes me want to weep or scream or both."

"I know, the lowest of the low. But Scout, between you and me? You can't get your hopes up too high, I'm sorry. The outlook is bleak at this point. I wish I could say otherwise, but I can't."

"I appreciate your being honest with me. It's just hard." She shrugged and began picking up containers and carrying them to the kitchen. Then, she paused and looked up at him. "Can you stay? I may be doing my rotisserie chicken impression trying to sleep tonight, but I'd still like to have you here."

"I would love to. If you can't sleep, we'll find a way to pass the time." He caught her by the waist and pulled her close. "Got any mad libs we can do?" Audrey laughed at that, and the sound filled in the hollows he'd been feeling all day.

"Wake up. You can't sleep here." The woman who had waited on Julius in the bar was standing by his car. He lifted his head and noticed the late hour. How long had he been sleeping, he wondered? Hannah would have a cow.

"Thanks," he nodded toward the woman before turning on the car and rolling up the windows. The air conditioning was slow to kick in, but he turned the fan to high, trying to blow off the last of the alcohol. Finally, he put the car into gear and turned back toward the highway. At that late hour, the roadway held less than a quarter of the traffic it had earlier, and he made time quickly. He pulled into the garage and shut off the car before scrubbing his hands over his face. He found an old tic tac in his shirt pocket and shoved it into his mouth. He knew it wouldn't cover up much, but what could he do?

When he got into the kitchen, it smelled pretty good. The light was still on over the stove, so he opened the oven and pulled out a foil-covered plate. He peeled the cover off and held it up close to his nose. Hmm. He gave it a minute in the microwave and then settled down to eat. Halfway through, he looked at the clock, 11:13. Damn, he had been out. He shoved the rest of the food down, put the plate and silverware into the dishwasher, and headed upstairs. He expected to find Hannah asleep in bed, but their room was empty when he got there. He stepped back out and eased open the door to the nursery. Hannah was asleep in the rocking chair, the baby resting in her arms, fast asleep as well. My God, he had forgotten how beautiful his wife was. He stood there soaking it in before moving forward and kissing her on the cheek.

"Come on to bed, love." She opened her eyes then and looked into his face. He wasn't quite sure what her expression meant, but gradually it transformed into a smile, and he kissed her again. Then, carefully, he reached under the tiny form and set it gently into the crib. Both of them held their breath for a second, but the baby continued to sleep. He took Hannah by the hand and led her back to their bedroom. "I'm sorry I was so late, dear." What the hell. He was so tired of lying he figured he'd just tell her the truth. "The highway was completely blocked when I was coming home, so I stopped at a bar and had a couple of drinks. When I got back to the car, I didn't think I was in any shape to drive home, so I decided to close my eyes for a while." He shrugged his shoulders before pulling her to him. "I should have called, I know. The time just got away from me. I'm sorry."

He looked down and was pleased to see the sweet look on her face. Maybe he should have tried telling the truth before this. She stood on her toes and brought her hands up around his neck. "I'm just glad that you're home now."

"Me, too," he smiled and lifted her into his arms and took the two of them to bed. They made love slowly and carefully, something they hadn't done in weeks. Then, with the lights out, he managed to put Mia and her butterfly tattoo out of mind.

"Order in the court." The judge tapped his gavel, and Audrey took a deep breath, forcing her shoulders back as she returned to the witness stand. The judge looked over at her. "You understand that you are still under oath, Ms. Markum?"

"Yes, your honor."

"Very well, Defense, are you ready to begin?"

"Your honor." Adams's attorney stepped up to the podium and looked directly at Audrey. "Ms. Markum. It's good to see you looking so well this morning."

Audrey chose not to answer but sat waiting for the first question.

"Now, Ms. Markum, you mentioned yesterday that there were several things that disturbed you in the spring?"

"Yes."

"Now, I understand that in your work for the police department, you must be present at some horrific crime scenes. Is that correct?"

"I've seen some things that were disturbing, yes."

"Yet we're to believe that you were worried about a lightbulb being out at your apartment?" She tilted her head and looked skeptically at the jury.

"Yes, I am a woman living alone in the city. I would be a fool not to pay attention to something like that."

"Very well then." She waved her hand in a dismissive gesture, and Audrey could feel the sweat forming along the hairline at the back of her neck. "Now, the next item you mentioned was a coffee shop, is that correct?"

"Yes, it is."

"You had a camera with you, a nice one, I presume, given your line of work?"

"Yes."

"And this is a camera that you're very familiar with, is that right?"

"Yes, it is."

"Then forgive me, but if you're a skilled photographer with a nice camera that you're very familiar with, why don't you have a photograph of my client if you did indeed see him?"

Audrey's eyes glanced over at Adams and saw the smirk playing across his lips. She averted her eyes quickly and looked again at the attorney. "I was taking photographs of very small, detailed items that morning, not people. When I spotted Mr. Adams in the window, I needed to adjust the zoom and, once I had, he was no longer there."

"Well then, it could have been anyone, correct?"

Audrey blinked but refused to lower her gaze. "Correct." She thought that the attorney looked a little surprised at her admission.

"All right. Now then, the next item you mentioned was an exchange at the market with Mr. Dhaliwal, I believe?"

"Yes."

"I believe he passed on a message to you from someone who said he was Gary Adams, a hello, is that right?"

Audrey felt a drip of sweat begin to slide down her neck. "That is correct."

"And someone sending a simple greeting, saying 'hi' to you?" She consulted her notepad. "This led you to feel 'terrified'?" She made broad air quote gestures with her hands and looked again at the jury. "And why was that?"

Audrey looked at Gabriel then, shocked that Adams's lawyer would ask her that. Gabriel had said that Adams's earlier conviction was not allowed in this trial, and she had answered the questions the day before with that in mind. Now, with a steady gaze and the beginning of a smile, he nodded once to let Audrey know that she should answer the question. "I remembered the name Gary Adams from when I was a child. He frightened me."

With that, the attorney suddenly seemed to realize that she'd made a tactical error in her questioning. She spoke quickly to try and cover it up. "Yes, now, all right then. Yesterday, you told the court about when you walked into the apartment across the street from your own."

"When I was marched into the apartment at gunpoint, you mean?"

The woman glanced up quickly and hardened her tone. "When you entered that apartment, you stated that there was a wooden chair in the middle of the room. Why should the jury care about a chair in the room of an apartment? I'm sure we all have chairs scattered around our apartments."

"The chair was in the middle of the kitchen and dining area. To the side, there was a round table with four matching chairs. There were three tall bar stools at the counter, and in the living room, there was a leather sofa and two leather recliners. I noticed the wooden chair because it didn't look right. It wasn't where it belonged."

"You mean where you thought it belonged."

"Objection, she already answered the question," Gabriel asserted.

"Sustained." The judge looked at the attorney and raised his hand to indicate she should continue.

"All right. Ms. Markum, of course, we were all shocked to see the photographs of you when you were hurt. It's just wonderful to see you looking so well now. Not a mark on you, huh? That's just so nice to see." She looked up at the judge then. "No more questions, your honor."

"Redirect, counselor?"

Gabriel nodded and replaced the woman at the podium. He mouthed the word 'sorry' at Audrey, and she lowered her head a fraction before raising her eyes to meet his. "Ms. Markum, the defense attorney made a big deal about how well you look today." He smiled. "I'm also very glad that you appear to be well. Can you tell the court whether all of your injuries have healed?"

Audrey looked at her father and then turned her gaze to the jury. "Physically, my wounds did heal. Unfortunately, the psychological ones remain."

"Can you explain?"

"I have panic attacks and night sweats. I find it very difficult some days to cross the threshold of my apartment building. My physician has diagnosed it as PTSD."

"That stands for Post-Traumatic Stress Disorder, is that correct?"

"Yes."

"And are there medications that you can take for that to cure it?"

"There are some. I tried a few right after the attack happened, but they didn't help all that much. Once my injuries had healed, things improved a bit."

"And recently?"

Audrey forced herself to look up, focusing on Gabriel as she spoke. "The panic attacks have gotten much worse as the trial approached. I'm again having trouble eating and sleeping and leaving my apartment building."

"And has it affected you professionally?"

"So far, I've managed to maintain my work schedule, although I leave myself additional time so that I can recover if there's an attack. I'm also planning to look for a new apartment."

"Thank you. Nothing further, your honor."

He banged his gavel and nodded at Audrey. "You may step down, Ms. Markum. We are in recess until 1:30." As he left, Audrey made her way to her father and fell into his arms once more. He held her tight, and then she stepped back as Gabriel came toward her.

He took both of her hands in his. "You were brilliant, Audrey. Well done."

"Really? I wasn't sure what to say when she asked me why his name scared me."

Gabriel grinned broadly before leaning close to whisper in her ear. "That's because she fucked up!" He leaned back. "Now the jury knows there was a connection, that you weren't a random person he scooped up off the street. You did great, believe me."

The crowd had left the room, but the main door opened, and Gabriel gestured for someone to come in. Audrey was thrilled to see Rod walking down the central aisle. "Right on time, detective," Gabriel announced.

Rod hugged Audrey in a swift embrace before stepping back to shake hands with the two men. "So, how'd it go? Am I up next?"

"She was terrific." Gabriel answered. "And yes, 1:30 is when we're due back. You'll be up first. Now, go and get some lunch and relax." He gently touched Audrey's shoulder before heading toward the main door.

Suddenly, the energy seemed to drain out of her, and she sat down on the nearest chair. "God, I'm exhausted. I don't ever want to have to go through that again."

Audrey's dad wrapped his arm around her shoulders. "You did great, my girl. I'm proud of you. Now let's get some lunch. I'm starving."

"Me too! I want my own sandwich today, Dad. I might even eat two!"

Rod was happy to follow Audrey and her father out the courthouse's back door and down the block to a sandwich shop. It took a little while to be waited on, but their drinks and meals came quickly after that, and the break provided a nice distraction after another morning spent spinning his wheels with Smitty. With the apartment search completed and the samples sent off for testing, there was little more to do than sit and wait for the results. Rod kept picturing Audrey's friend Sandy and her husband and wished more than ever that he had some tiny bit of hope to offer them. He finished his sandwich but left most of his chips untouched as his nerves about testifying started to take over.

All too quickly, it was time to return to court. Audrey and her dad phoned to check in with her mother, and then the three of them entered the courtroom. Rod took a seat at the end of the row next to Audrey. He noticed that she was holding his hand as well as her father's, and he sent up a quick prayer that the whole ordeal would finish today.

"Order, order." The bailiff called the court to order, and the room grew quiet. Gabriel stepped up to the podium.

"Your honor, I'd like to call Detective Stanley Rodriguez to the stand."

Rod felt a quick squeeze from Audrey and saw the slight grin as the name Stanley was pronounced. Then he stepped up and was sworn in. "Detective Rodriguez."

Rod lifted his hand, "Rod, please."

"Rod, can you describe your current position to us?"

"I'm a detective, first-class, with the Pittsburgh police department, homicide division."

"Thank you. And I understand that you are acquainted with Ms. Markum?"

"Yes."

"Professionally? I understand that she works for your department."

"Yes, professionally, and personally. We have been dating since this spring."

"Were you acquainted with Ms. Markum during the week in question?"

"Yes, we were beginning to go out then. We had dinner together at a restaurant that Wednesday evening, and on Thursday, we had dinner together at her apartment."

"Were you aware at the time of Ms. Markum's misgivings regarding the apartment building where she was living?"

"Yes, and I shared them. When I went to her apartment, I was concerned about the missing light as well as the building's external security system."

"What was wrong with the system?"

"It was old, had probably been there for a decade or more, and I assumed that everybody and his brother probably knew the combination."

"Did Ms. Markum also mention to you her fears regarding the defendant?"

"Yes, she told me that she thought she had seen him at a coffee shop. She also told me about the incident at the market."

"Now, later on that week, did you also have plans?"

"Yes, we were supposed to have lunch together on Saturday."

"And when did you become concerned?"

Rod glanced over at Audrey and forced himself to take a long breath. "I was expecting her to call me early that morning so that we could decide where and when to meet."

"And did she call?"

"No, and I had been trying to call her, but it kept going to voice mail."

"And when did you hear from her?"

"I finally received a text around nine-thirty in the morning."

"And what did it say?"

"Help, it just said help. I tried to call her back, but she texted that she couldn't hear well enough to use the phone. She texted me that she was in her apartment and to come quickly."

"And did you?"

"Hell yes. I used the light on my car and got there as fast as I could."

"And what did you discover when you arrived?"

"Audrey looked like she'd been hit by a truck. I started to call an ambulance."

"Started to?"

Rod nodded . "She was frightened about her parents and wanted to make sure that they were safe. She didn't want to take the time to go to the hospital first."

"What did you do then?"

"I got dispatch to send units to her folks' house and another to pick us up at her apartment. Audrey gave the police a description of Adams, and we made good time. We were almost there when an ambulance came up behind us, and we had to pull over to let it go past. By the time we arrived at her parents' house, it was all over."

"Thank you, Detective. That is all." Rod looked up as Gabriel returned to his seat and Adams's attorney stood up.

"No questions at this time."

"Very well." The judge responded. "Mr. Perez?"

As Rod returned to his seat, Gabriel stepped back up to the podium. "Your honor, at this time, I'd like to call my last witness, Officer John Chao."

Rod settled into his seat as Chao took the stand and was sworn in. With his trim build, black, flattop haircut, and snappy dress uniform, Rod thought the young officer looked like a Hollywood version of a cop. He decided he liked that.

"Officer, it is my understanding that you were in one of the units that responded to the call at Ms. Markum's parents' house. Is that correct?"

"Yes."

"Now, can you tell us specifically what happened that Saturday morning in May?"

"My partner and I responded to a call out of Zone Six that an armed man was heading to a home on Sycamore."

"Was your car the only one responding?"

"No. There was a second cruiser. Using the victim's description, the other car spotted the assailant and directed us to help them block him in. Once Adams spotted us, he took a shot at my partner." He jutted his chin out toward Adams. "He missed. The other unit returned fire and hit Adams, wounding him."

"This happened quickly. I take it? How was the other car able to identify Adams as the suspect?"

Rod watched as Chao reached into his back pocket and pulled out a folded sheet of paper. "I thought you might ask. This is the description we received over the radio. May I read it?"

Gabriel looked at the judge, and as he nodded, Gabriel nodded in turn. "Please."

"*She says he has hazel eyes, curly hair that's medium brown and comes down past his collar, but the last she saw him, he had on an old, red Phillies cap. He weighs at least forty more pounds than he did in our photograph. He's got on a dark blue T-shirt with a medium blue plaid flannel shirt over it, blue jeans, and black running shoes.*" He looked up then. "I was so impressed with the description that I had dispatch print it out for me." He grinned over at Audrey for a second. "She's got quite an eye for detail, let me tell you."

"Once the suspect was secured, what did you find in his vehicle?"

"It was a rental car, and in the back was a duffle bag that contained clothing and some food items, as well as several lengths of rope and a loaded handgun. It also held a brown leather camera bag that we determined was the victim's. It contained her camera and lenses as well as a set of hearing aids."

"Thank you. Now, Officer, I understand you also accompanied the team to the apartment where Ms. Markum was held. Is that correct?"

"Yes, I supervised the team of technicians that went in."

"And how did the apartment look? What did they find?"

"They dusted for prints everywhere but found only partials, nothing conclusive."

"And the heavy wooden chair that Ms. Markum described being in the center of the room?"

"It was at a desk in a back bedroom that had a computer on it."

"Thank you." Gabriel nodded before returning his gaze to the judge.

Gabriel returned to his seat, and Adams's attorney stepped to the podium once again. "Officer Chao. I just wanted to clarify one or two things. When you arrived at the apartment, there was no chair in the center of the room the way Ms. Markum described, is that correct?"

"Yes."

"And no fingerprints that your department concluded belonged to my client?"

"Correct.

"Thank you. That is all."

The judge looked at Gabriel, and Rod watched as he stood at his table. "Nothing further, your honor. The prosecution rests its case."

"Very well. The court is adjourned for the day. We will begin in the morning with the defense."

Chairs shuffled as people stood and moved to exit the room. Audrey and her father remained seated, and Gabriel came over to talk with them once the room had emptied. "So, folks, how are you feeling?"

Rod looked at Audrey, who spoke first. "Relieved, I guess. What happens now? Will we have to testify again tomorrow?"

"Neither of you is named on the defense's list of witnesses, so no. Frankly, I'm not sure what the defense will do now. They can't push on the coincidence line since she let the cat out of the bag that you knew who he was. Her only choice may be to call Adams to the stand, and I can't picture that going very well." He stood then. "You don't have to be here anymore if you don't want to, Audrey. You did a great job. You really did." He turned toward Rod. "You too, Detective. Nice work." He snapped his briefcase shut and turned to head up the aisle. "Have a good night, everyone."

"You too, Gabriel, thank you again!" Audrey called up to him.

"Well, we did it, Scout." Rod stood, looked down, and pulled Audrey to her feet. "We did the very best we could, and now we have to let it go. It's out of our hands at this point. Anyone want to get a . . ." His phone vibrated in his pocket, and he pulled it out. "It's Smitty. Give me just a second."

He stepped away from the group and clicked on the call. "Hey, we just got done. Want to meet us for a drink?"

"How'd it go?"

"Good, I think. We're just glad that our part is done. What's up?"

"We got a weird-ass call just this afternoon. I thought you might be interested. You know Dave's Used Cars, up north of the city off Route 19?"

"No, can't say I do."

"Well, it's about two steps up from a junkyard, not much to speak of. Anyway, the owner called Properties today to say that he's missing a car."

"Okay."

"Here's the weird thing, though. He's got an extra one just like it."

"How'd that happen? A paperwork mix-up or something? He get the VIN wrong?"

"That's what I figured. Dispatch sent a uniform out to check on it, write it up. She just called. It's got no keys, and the console's been cleaned out, but she found the base to a car seat on the floor of the back seat."

"Did she have the car towed in?"

"No, she remembered our missing baby case and got suspicious, decided to wait and have a team look at it there. You interested?"

"Holy shit, yes. Text me the address. I'll meet you there." He looked at his watch. "Give me fifteen, okay?"

"Will do." The call clicked off, and Rod felt it vibrate again with the texted address. He walked back to Audrey and her dad. "I'm sorry, I'm not going to be able to get that drink after all."

Audrey's father put his hand out to shake Rod's. "Me either, I'm afraid, I feel like I'd better get home. We'll get together soon, though, okay?"

"Will do, Mr. Markum."

"Oh, Mitch, please. Audrey, hon," he wrapped his daughter in a hug. "Do you want me to give you a ride home? Are you planning to come back tomorrow?"

"I haven't decided whether I'll come tomorrow or not, but you don't have to. I'll be fine. I appreciate everything you've done." She looked over at Rod. "I don't think I need a ride, do I?"

Rod didn't know whether it was a good idea to bring her along or not, but for some reason, he didn't want to let her out of his sight yet. He could admit that having all of those images from the attack brought back so clearly had left him feeling a little rattled. "Actually, I'd be glad to have her with me if you don't mind."

"That's fine. Audrey, will you call me if you change your mind? I don't mind coming tomorrow."

"Sure thing, and, Dad, thank you again for everything." Audrey gave her father a quick kiss on the cheek and watched him walk away before turning her attention back to Rod. "What's up?"

"Smitty has a lead, a used car dealer. Want to ride along with me?"

"Sure, anything to clear all of this out of my head. I'm going to be going nuts waiting to hear what happens next."

"Great, Smitty's going to meet us there."

Half an hour later, Smitty pulled into the used car lot. Deke was right. It wasn't much more than a junkyard with long rows of beat-up vehicles stretching back toward a tall, chain-link fence. There was a black and white and a tow truck parked at the end of the last row, and Smitty made his way toward them. The officer tucked her phone away and put out her hand. "How's it going?"

He touched his shirt front. "I'm Smitty. Deke gave me a call. You Laura?"

She shook his hand confidently despite her youthful appearance. "Laura Katz."

"I appreciate you making the call, Laura. Tell me what's up."

"The owner called in this morning to say that the wrong car was in his lot. He didn't have any keys for it, and he has no idea what happened to the one he's supposed to have." She gestured toward the driver's door. "Owner got the door open for me, but I stopped him then and started to search it." She pointed at a white, square plastic base that still had cellophane around the side of it sitting on the passenger seat.

"Did you pop the trunk?"

"I decided to wait. I'd already called the tow but thought maybe you'd want to have a look at the car here before it gets moved."

"Smart. Okay, grab some gloves and then pop the trunk for me."

She reached into her car and pulled out two pairs of latex gloves, handing one to him and putting the other pair on herself. Then, she reached down beside the driver's seat and pushed the button. Together, they walked back to the rear of the car as Smitty pulled a small flashlight from his pocket. He looked over at Laura. "I don't see anything on the outside, but it stinks a bit, don't you think?"

She nodded, and the two of them peered in as Smitty shown the light around the interior of the trunk. A dark, brown residue coated one side of the torn carpet that lined the trunk. Smitty carefully lifted a plastic-covered wrench set and noticed that it too was coated. He set it down gently and turned to Laura. "You did a great job spotting this and giving us a call." He saw Rod's truck pulling into the lot. "Do you mind letting the tow go but giving the lab a call so they can send some techs out?"

"Sure thing." As she walked toward the tow truck, Smitty stepped forward to meet Rod and Audrey.

He bent to give Audrey a quick hug. "Well, you look like you're still in one piece. It's good to see you."

"Thank you, Smitty. I'm just glad to be out of there."

Rod stepped toward the car, and Smitty fell into step beside him. "What do you think? Is it our car?"

"I think it's possible." He gestured toward where Laura sat in her front seat of the cruiser, talking with dispatch. "She did a great job calling us in. Come and look." Smitty showed him the car seat base first before stepping back toward the trunk and shining his light once again."

"Shit, looks like blood to me." Rod leaned over and then straightened back up. "Smells like it too. You got a hit on the VIN?"

"Waiting on it now."

Laura walked back over to them. "Techs are about twenty minutes out. You want me to stay?"

Smitty peeled off his gloves and shook her hand again. "No, thanks. We'll wait for them. Great work today."

"Sure thing. See you around."

As she was pulling out, Audrey stepped forward. "What's going on?" She looked from one man to the other, and Smitty gestured toward the car.

"We think this could be the car that was used to move Mia Novak's body." He pointed at the car seat base. "That was on the floor in the back seat."

Smitty's phone rang then, and he gestured in the air for a pen. Audrey pulled a pad and pencil out of her purse and handed it to him. He wrote quickly, his breath catching as the clerk read out the name and address of the owner. Then he turned to Rod and Audrey. "Julius Dudnyk. They're running his name through the system now."

"My God, Jewels," Audrey whispered, and both men nodded.

42

It was still dark when Julius's alarm went off, but when he reached beside him, Hannah was already out of bed. He got up, pulled a fresh shirt out of the closet, and grabbed the pants he'd hung on the chair the night before. Then, he headed into the shower. He stood under the warm water, gradually turning up the temperature until it was almost scalding his back. He twisted his head back and forth, hoping the heat would work some of the stress out of his neck. But it was no use. He turned off the water and toweled dry, then dressed and headed down to breakfast. Once again, the kitchen smelled wonderful.

The baby was in a new swing with some sort of tune playing while Hannah stood cracking eggs into a red plastic bowl. She turned around as soon as he walked in, a broad smile across her face. "Good morning," she beamed up at him.

"Good morning. You're up early."

"Oh, new mothers are always up early. Do you have time to eat? The bacon's just done, and I was going to scramble some eggs, maybe put a little bit of cheese in?"

"Sure," he poured himself a cup of coffee and carried it over to the table. He sat down across from where the baby was swinging, observing her. Maybe she wasn't quite as red and pinched looking today, he thought. And she wasn't crying. Instead, she seemed to be looking around the room. He turned then and watched as Hannah adjusted the flame under the small skillet and moved a wide spatula back and forth, adding a bit of salt and pepper. God, it all looked so fucking normal, he thought. He had everything that he'd set out to get, a baby, a smile on his wife's face, everything. But there was no way it would last, not after what happened with Mia, what he did to Mia, he told himself. There was sunshine coming in the kitchen window now, and it looked as though it was going to be a beautiful day. "Let's go somewhere today, Hannah. Take Joy with us."

"You mean like a picnic?" She spooned the eggs onto a plate and set them in front of him, adding strips of bacon and a piece of buttered toast.

Julius wrapped his arm around her waist. "Sure, a picnic. Why not? I've got some days coming at work. I'll give them a call when I'm done eating." He released her then and started to eat as she began humming along with the children's song that the swing was playing. He watched as she took her sponge, wiping the edges of the stove and around the counters. It looked normal, he thought, normal wiping up, not the rigid, OCD routine that she usually went through. He'd known having a baby was going to be good for her.

Once Hannah brought the baby back downstairs, dressed and in her baby seat, Julius panicked. Crap, he didn't have the base for the carrier, and Hannah would know it wasn't the right car. What could he do? He stepped out onto the front porch and took out his phone, typed in a search, and then called the first car service that came up. Thank God they provided car seats. He went inside and called to Hannah out in the kitchen. "Hannah, the car's been acting up, so I've called a service for us. They even have car seats available." She walked into the living room then, and he studied her face. She had the same expression that he'd seen the night before, but he still couldn't understand what it meant. Did she know something was wrong? She paused and looked at him before setting down the seat and turning toward the stairs.

"I think she might need a hat and some sunscreen. I'll just go up and get it." When she returned in a few minutes, her expression had changed back to a smile again, and he remained puzzled. Then a car honked, and they were soon out the door.

Audrey didn't know what to think when they pulled into the used car lot. What she couldn't figure out was whether finding the car would help them find Rosey. With Mia dead and the vehicle dumped, surely whoever had taken the baby would be long gone. A plane, a train, even a rental car could have taken whoever it was and Rosey out of the city, out of the state, maybe even farther.

But they had a name now. Jewels, Julius. Rod and Smitty spent some more time examining the car and then talking with the techs when they arrived. Audrey tried to listen and keep out of everyone's way at the same time. Finally, Smitty got back into his car, and Rod joined Audrey in his. "What does this mean, Rod? Can it help us find Rosey?"

"We certainly hope so. Smitty's taking his driver's license photo back to the cousin's bar to see if anyone there recognizes him. We also sent a car out to keep an eye on his house. If Smitty gets confirmation that it's our man, then we're heading to the house too."

"Do you think Rosey's there?"

Rod turned to face her in the seat and rested his hand on her shoulder before reaching up and cupping her cheek. "Audrey, you can't get your hopes up. I'm sorry. The odds that he still has Rosey or that she's all right are pretty slim. You know that, right?" Audrey nodded. "Would you like me to take you home while we wait? We could pick up some more take-out. Or would you rather be on your own after all of this today?" He gestured at the area around them.

"I'm ready to go home, but yeah, let's pick up some food on the way." She paged through a couple of restaurant menus on her phone before they settled on one, and she placed the order. They stopped at a favorite barbecue place on the way back into town, and the bag felt like it held enough food for a small army. Audrey settled it on the floor in front of her and pulled out a fry. "We're going to be eating this for days."

Rod looked over at her and made a silly, lascivious grin.

"I like a little barbecue for breakfast, myself."

Audrey laughed. "Really? I'm happy with breakfast for dinner but *not* the other way around." She rested her hand on his knee. "But I would love it if you stayed over again."

They had just gotten inside and started pulling out plates when Rod's phone buzzed. He answered it quickly but said little. "Tomorrow morning?" He paused, looking out the window as he listened. "Can the car keep watch there overnight?" He nodded and confirmed an appointment for eight in the morning before hanging up and pocketing the phone.

"What's up?"

Rod added some extra hot sauce to his plate before carrying it to the table. "The busboy is out of town with his family, won't be back until late tonight. The bartender, Mia's cousin? He didn't recognize the guy. So Smitty and I are going to meet at the kid's house in the morning. If he says Julius is the guy, then we'll get a tactical team and head out to his house. In the meantime, the captain agreed to keep a patrol on site and let us know if anything happens tonight."

"Then once again, we wait. Geez, this is hard, and I feel so bad for Sandy and her family."

"Have you talked to your mom lately?"

"No, we traded a few texts, but she didn't have any news. She was planning to stay at the house until Oscar got home from work. She said that Sandy and her mom are both a little weepy, and baby Martha is having trouble sleeping." Audrey looked up at Rod. "I think she misses Rosey. She would always rest her hand on Rosey's arm or leg or whatever she could reach. It was like she was looking out for her."

"That's tough. Poor little thing can't understand anything at all."

"Oh, and Mom said she saw on the news that there's going to be a service for Mia next weekend."

"Yeah, the department found her parents' address over near Philly, and they agreed to come and take care of everything."

"I can't imagine having to bury your kid at any age."

"Me neither."

Their conversation drifted back to the court case and the day's testimony. Finally, Audrey asked, "what would their defense even look like, Rod? What can they say? She already goofed and let everyone know that I recognized his name. I don't understand how that gets walked back."

"Well, the judge can tell the jury to disregard it, but I don't think that ever works. If Gabriel had made the mistake, Adams could ask for a mistrial, but since their side did it?" He shrugged. "I don't know what they'll do. Are you going to go back and watch? Do you have to be there?"

She shook her head. "No, Gabriel said I didn't have to. I am curious about what they'll say, though. Why don't we set the alarm so that we're up early? Then, you can get to your appointment with Smitty, and I can take a few minutes to decide whether I want to go to court or not. Maybe I'll give my dad a call, although I don't much feel like making him come back into town again."

"He wouldn't mind."

"I know. I just hate feeling like a big baby."

"Audrey," he ran his finger down the length of her nose, a line that was not quite as straight as it had been. "You are one of the toughest people I've ever met, and I'm a policeman. If you go or not, if you go by yourself or ask your dad, it doesn't matter. You're Audrey Markum, and you saved your own life. Look that bastard in the eye and see if he doesn't blink first."

"Wow, you may be the best boyfriend ever." Audrey leaned over and kissed him before taking her plate to the sink. She divided the leftover food up into a couple of containers and put it all away in the refrigerator. Then she grabbed the carton of cappuccino ice cream and two spoons. "Want to watch a movie?"

Rod put his plate and silverware in the dishwasher before turning to Audrey and pulling her against him. She wrapped her arms around him and held tight before touching the edge of the carton to his neck. "Yikes, girl!" They both dissolved into laughter. "Just for that, I get to pick the movie."

"Sounds fair to me, but I get to hold the ice cream carton."

"Deal."

Audrey thought they did well, making it halfway through the movie before they ditched the empty carton and headed to bed. It was a lame Rom-Com anyway, and in her mind, the real thing always outdid the movie version.

Her phone alarm buzzed and blinked in the faint light of morning. They spooned together briefly but then forced themselves to get moving. It might turn out to be a big day, Audrey thought, for them both. Once the coffee was ready, they stood at the counter and ate quickly before heading out. In the middle of the night, Audrey had awakened, and as she lay there trying to get back to sleep without disturbing Rod, she made a decision. She would see it through. Rod was right. There was nothing Adams could do to her now. When Rod was ready, she caught a ride over with him and sat waiting on the metal bench outside the courtroom. She was early, but that just meant she didn't have to fight her way through the reporters. She pulled a book up on her phone and read until it was time for court to reconvene.

It seemed silly, but Rod found himself feeling proud of Audrey as she headed into the courthouse. He'd meant what he said the night before. She was tough. My God, she had been hurt so badly. It still made him feel sick when he pictured her that morning, the way she looked and sounded on their desperate rush out to her parents' house. He knew that the PTSD was serious, but he also had faith that she would come to terms with it, would find a way to heal from it the way she had with her physical injuries. He only hoped that seeing the trial through would make that easier, not harder.

He put it all out of his mind, though, as he pulled up to the curb in front of the busboy's place. Smitty had texted him the address, and Rod saw him now, leaning against the side of his car waiting for Rod.

"Ready?"

"You bet." Carlos Santiago and his mother lived in a small apartment building that Rod thought looked a lot like Audrey's. Smitty had blown up the photograph from Julius Dudnyk's driver's license, and he held it in his hand as they mounted the steps together. They rang the bell and waited, the sound of footsteps growing closer. Finally, a woman in her late thirties answered, and Rod saw Carlos standing just behind her.

"Good morning, Ma'am." Smitty began, his badge open in his hand. "I'm Detective Smith, and this is my partner Detective Rodriguez. We'd like to have a word with your son Carlos if we could."

The woman seemed hesitant and moved so that her body was blocking their view of the boy. "Is something wrong? My son's a good boy."

"We know that Ma'am. He's not in any trouble at all. We just want to ask him about a man he might have seen when he was working at the bar. If we could come in, or if you two would like to step out, you're welcome to stay right here with us as we talk."

The woman's shoulders relaxed then, and she and her son stepped out into the hallway, the light from the apartment spilling over their shoulders. Smitty held up the photograph of Julius. "Carlos, we were wondering if you recognize this man, if you might have seen him at the bar."

The young man took the photograph and held it where his mother could see it as well before nodding. "Yeah, that's the guy, the Jewels guy that I saw with Mia." He looked up then, a frightened expression on his face. "Did he . . ."

Rod answered. "We don't know anything about him Carlos, we just wanted to check with you to make sure that that's who you saw Mia with that Thursday evening. Are you sure?"

"Yeah, I recognize him. I told you he was too old for her, didn't I?"

Smitty took the photograph and folded it back into his pocket before reaching out to shake Carlos's hand. "Thank you, Carlos. We appreciate your help." Then he shook his mother's hand as well. "Thank you too, Ma'am. We appreciate you letting us talk with him."

She smiled and then stepped back inside the apartment, ushering Carlos in ahead of her.

Rod and Smitty returned to the curb, pausing beside Smitty's car. "Did you hear anything back from the patrol last night?"

Smitty pulled out his phone and scrolled through his texts. "Yeah, here it is. The subject and a woman returned to the house around seven-thirty last night." Rod looked up then. "They had an infant in a carrier with them."

"Mother fucker. Do we know if they have kids of their own? Do you think that's Rosey? You think they kept the baby for themselves?"

"We didn't find any record of kids, but it's a tricky thing to search for, especially if they're not school-aged yet. God knows we don't have the time to sit around going through city birth records. We need to move.

Let's get back and put a team together. I don't want to take any chances on this."

In answer, Rod was already hurrying to his truck, and the two vehicles made good time getting back to the station. They met in the captain's office along with four uniformed cops. The patrol car that was keeping watch on the house was on speakerphone. "*No movement here yet.*" The comment crackled as the captain turned to Rod and Smitty. "What's the plan, boys?"

Smitty answered first. "We don't want to tip anyone off, Cap, so we've got to come in quiet."

"Agreed."

Smitty used the man's computer to pull up a map of the residential area. "We need units here and here," he indicated a distance on either side of the house. "Then another unit here in the back." He gestured at the street that paralleled the one the Dudnyk's house was on. "We have to be careful. Remember, there's a baby inside, and we have no idea what kind of resistance we might run into."

"All right." The captain nodded. "Make sure everyone's got their vests on. We'll move in ten."

The group turned and headed to their desks and lockers to gather the necessary gear. Five minutes later, Rod and Smitty were in Rod's truck, ready to lead the group. "I know we've got back up." Smitty began. "But what are we going to do first? Just knock on the door?"

Rod looked over at his partner. "I guess that's as good a way to start as any."

"Well, say these folks just open up the door to us. How are we going to know if the baby is theirs or not? Will you recognize Rosey?" Smitty asked.

"I've seen her but, honestly, babies all look kind of the same to me." Rod flipped through the images on his phone and came up with one of the photographs that Sandy had sent them. He studied it and then turned it to face Smitty. "Do you think we can tell from this?"

"I know I couldn't." Suddenly both men turned to face each other and spoke at the same time.

"Audrey."

"Scout."

Rod began texting on his phone. "Look, I'll see if she can get free. You call the captain and see if he can give us a head start." Smitty was still waiting for the station to pick up when Audrey responded. "*It's over. Closing arguments done. Judge giving the jury instructions now.*"

He answered. "*If you're free, we need you. Can Smitty and I come pick you up?*"

"*Sure, be out front.*"

"Okay, Captain says he'll give us a ten-minute head start. Then they're moving out."

45

It was getting dark when the driver dropped them off after their picnic. Julius was pleased with how the whole day had gone. They had picked one of the riverfront parks and, with the baby in the stroller, were able to walk along the trails and enjoy the beautiful day. Hannah had packed food as well as several baby bottles, so they took their time, shifting from the sun to the shade as the day grew warmer. Finally, in the late afternoon, they made their way out of the park back toward the downtown area, where they found a restaurant that was open early for dinner.

Julius was surprised that the baby stayed pretty calm all day. Of course, she fussed when she was hungry or needed a change, but the horrible shrieking seemed to have stopped. Hannah truly was a wonderful mother, he thought. Even in the restaurant, somehow, she managed to balance her food and the baby while making it look easy. As they were finishing their dinner, she needed to use the restroom, so he held the baby and prayed that she would remain quiet.

He still wasn't quite sure what he was doing, but he knew he didn't want to drop her, so he hooked his heels into the crosspiece of his chair, which brought his knees up. Then he rested the baby in his lap. It was interesting how she seemed to be looking all around her, taking it all in, the lights and the noise. But then she seemed to stop and look at him. It was as if she was searching his face almost. He knew that she didn't recognize him yet, and he held his breath as he imagined the scream that would follow.

Instead, she smiled, and his eyes filled with tears. What had he done? This was someone's child. As happy as it made Hannah, they had no right to this baby. And Mia? What a price she had paid. Too much. It was too much. He had to say something to Hannah. He had to make it right.

When they got home, the baby was awake again, so Hannah fed her and then gave her a bath in a small pink tub that Julius had never seen before. He stood in the doorway watching as the baby cooed and his wife sang to her softly. It seemed as though the kid liked the water. Once she was dried and dressed for the night, Hannah sat rocking her as he continued to watch. She half read, half recited the child a story about a moon, and within minutes the baby was asleep again. Julius gestured for her to lay the baby in the crib and then took Hannah's hand as they headed downstairs to the living room.

"Are you hungry?" she asked.

"No, I'm fine. Come sit with me." She followed him over to the sofa and then sat down close beside him.

"Such a wonderful day. Thank you, Julius."

"It was special, wasn't it?" It hung in the air then, everything that he ought to say, every confession he needed to make. The drive back to the house had unexpectedly gone past the used car dealership, and he'd spotted a tow truck and a police cruiser as they went by. It was time to act, to say something to her. He played with sentence after sentence in his head, but nothing sounded right. Should he tell her about the baby or about Mia too? And did he need to tell her about the sex or just about the killing? Jesus. He had no words. He heard his wife's even breathing then and realized that she'd fallen asleep waiting for him to decide what to say. "They're coming for her," he whispered. But Hannah's breathing didn't change. He sat for a long time, listening and watching her before he dozed off himself. Hours later, he woke up, and she was gone, so he headed up the stairs. He checked the nursery first and saw that the child was sleeping. Then he walked into their bedroom, stripped off his clothes, and climbed into bed. But he kept to his side of it and managed not to wake his wife.

Julius slept fitfully and was surprised to see the light coming in once he woke up for good. It was past seven, and he could hear Hannah in the kitchen. The time had come, he told himself, as he stepped into a cold shower and then into fresh clothes. The baby was back in her swing, and

Hannah was at the stove when he walked in. He walked up behind her and wrapped his arms around her waist. "Something smells good."

She turned to face him and smiled, reaching to kiss him before turning back to the stove. "I thought you might like some pancakes this morning. They just need a minute more."

Julius stood beside her and watched, entranced as tiny bubbles formed and popped on the surface of the pancakes. So that was how you knew when they were done. He'd always wondered. He caught his brain wandering then and forced himself to focus. He had to talk to her, and he had to do it now. She transferred the pancakes to two plates that were waiting beside the stove. Before she could pour out more batter, he reached around her and turned off the burner. "Honey, we need to talk." He carried the plates over to the table and set them down, then pulled out the chair for his wife. Once she was seated, he angled his chair to face her, reached for her hands, and held them in his. "You must know. I never meant to hurt anyone, especially not you."

He searched Hannah's face but couldn't make out her expression. She just seemed to be watching him, waiting.

"All I ever wanted was for you to be happy. You are a wonderful mother, I've seen that. But . . ."

"What is it, Julius?" She was holding herself rigid, he noticed, expecting the blow that he was about to deliver.

"They're going to come for her, for Joy." He gestured toward the swing, which had wound down and gone silent, with the baby fast asleep inside. Hannah pulled her hands back and folded them into a tight ball, the knuckles white on top.

"She's the baby from the daycare center, isn't she?"

He was confused. "You know? How long have you known?" He leaned back away from her.

"For a while. Didn't you think I'd hear about it? Recognize her from the news?"

"And you didn't say anything?"

"What could I say?" She turned toward the child. "I had everything I ever wanted."

"What do we do now?" The question hung in the air between them, along with the scent of pancakes and the sound of birds from a nearby window. Then, abruptly, she stood and walked out of the room. He could hear her going upstairs, rummaging around for something. He waited, completely unsure what to do or say.

She returned and set four prescription bottles on the table between them. "What's that?" he asked.

"Sleeping pills. I've been saving them. Every time it looked like we'd get a baby, and then it fell through, I planned to take them."

"What are you saying, Hannah?"

"Is there any way that we could run? That we could hide from what's coming?"

He hung his head and shook it gently back and forth before looking back up at her. "I don't see how."

"Then what choice do we have? Julius, I know what you've done, or at least I can guess at it, and I don't care. I've been happy. I called her Joy because that's what she brought me. Yesterday was wonderful. Let's leave it at that."

He was shocked as she poured syrup on the side of the plate, took a bite of pancake and dipped it in, and ate it. Julius ate a few bites of his, too, and then she began opening the bottles. She counted out a good number for herself, more than doubled it for him, and set each handful on a napkin.

"Are you sure, Hannah? You shouldn't have to pay for my mistakes."

"Julius, all I want is to go first." She looked over at the baby. "I want to fall asleep holding my girl. Then you can put her in her crib and take yours. It's not too much to ask, you know." It was the least he could do. She carefully picked up the baby in one arm and collected the pills and her glass of orange juice in the other. He walked behind her, carrying his own as she made her way up the stairs.

In the nursery, Hannah handed the baby to Julius while she settled into the wooden rocker. She poured the pills into her mouth and drank the glass of juice in a motion that was so quick Julius couldn't believe what he'd seen. Then she put the glass on the floor by the chair and held out her arms. He handed the baby to her and then knelt on the floor beside the two of them. It didn't take long before Hannah's eyes began to close and he heard a brief, quiet gurgling sound before she fell silent.

He rested his hand on her knee and waited. When her left hand fell away from the baby, he eased the child away and set her in the crib. Then he took his own handful of pills and washed them down with the acrid juice. It was hard to swallow so many, and for a moment, he was afraid he'd throw up all over his wife. But he finished the glass and then knelt on the floor again, this time resting his head in his wife's lap. He thought that perhaps he could hear the baby starting to cry, but he couldn't hold onto the thought. "Hannah," he whispered, and the scent of her filled his nose and mind.

46

Audrey felt a little bit exposed sitting in the courtroom without her father or Rod beside her. She put her purse on the seat beside her so that no one could get too close. Just as the judge was walking in, a young man sidled into the row, startling her. She could see the press tag hanging out of his back pocket, so she turned in her seat, angling herself away from his prying eyes. The bailiff called the court to order, and the judge banged his gavel. "Defense, you may proceed at this time."

Adams's attorney, today in a dark brown, tailored suit, stepped up to the microphone. Audrey noticed that she seemed a little more put together, her hair pulled back in a neat bun, her notes in a tidy stack. "Thank you, your honor. I'd like to call my client, Mr. Gary Adams, to the stand." Audrey noticed that he, too, was well dressed and put together. It gave her a shiver to see him walk up and swear to tell the truth. She focused her gaze on the attorney and tried to avoid looking at Adams.

"Mr. Adams, can you please tell the court your whereabouts on the Wednesday in question?"

"I was in Butler, out at my sister's."

"So, you were not in a coffee shop in Ms. Markum's neighborhood that day?"

"Nah, no way. I wouldn't go to one of those places. You know how much they charge for a cup of coffee? Everyone sitting around with their computers, taking up every available table, sitting there . . ."

"Yes, I see." She quickly stepped in to interrupt his rant. "You were not at the coffee shop on Wednesday. Now, we've been told by several people that you were in a neighborhood market on that Thursday. Is that correct?"

"Yeah, I had to pick up some soup."

"And did you give the shopkeeper a message for Ms. Markum?"

"Sure, I said to tell her hi." Audrey saw him glance toward her then with a sick sort of grin on his face. She made herself meet his gaze but didn't allow her face to register any kind of response.

"And how did you happen to know Ms. Markum to say hello to her?"

"I got a job as a bouncer at a club over on Liberty. I met her there a couple of days before. I found a place to stay in the neighborhood, and I wanted to be friendly."

"But Mr. Adams, your encounter with Ms. Markum in the apartment wasn't friendly at all, was it?"

"Aw, no. I feel bad about that. At the club, she told me that she liked things a little rough, you know the type. Turned out she didn't like it so much after all. Probably she was just one of those women who reads about rough stuff, books like that Gray one, and thinks they're into it. Comes down to it, though, they don't really have the guts for it."

"You're saying that the injuries Ms. Markum received were the result of a sexual encounter? You didn't abduct her and take her to your place?"

"Abduct her? Oh, hell no. We had a date. She came to me. She'd had a bit to drink before she got there, and when I saw she wasn't really into it, I left her there to sleep it off."

"She was alive when you left? You made sure of this?"

"Of course, she was just a bit drunk, is all." Audrey felt her stomach churning at the list of lies he was spewing.

"Now, after you left the apartment, where did you go?"

"I took a drive, stopped, and got some breakfast. It was a nice day, so I decided to drive out through my old neighborhood. I'd been away, and I wanted to see how the place had changed."

"You had a handgun in your bag, is that right? Why was that?"

"Hey, you never know these days. Pays to protect yourself, I always say."

"Yesterday, Officer Chao testified that you fired at his partner. Is that correct?"

"Well yeah, that cop car came right up at me, scared the shit out of me. Sorry, scared the crap out of me. I saw a gun, so I fired mine first." He leaned back and spread his hands wide. "It's not like I hit him or anything."

"And in fact, it was you who was shot, is that correct?"

"You're damn right I was." He began to pull at his shirt. "I can show you the . . ."

Again, she stepped in to interrupt him. "That's just fine, no need for that, Mr. Adams." She looked up at the judge. "That is all, your honor."

"Very well. Counselor?"

Audrey watched as Gabriel replaced her at the podium and puzzled about what he would say. "Mr. Adams, can you please state your age for the court?"

"Sure. I'm 52."

"And you say that you met Ms. Markum at a bar and that she mentioned liking . . ." He gestured with his hands as he spoke. "The rough stuff, is that right?"

"You got it." Audrey couldn't believe the swagger that had entered his voice.

"You also stated that Ms. Markum was drunk on the night in question. Is that right?"

"As a skunk."

Gabriel reached back to the table, where he picked up a form that Audrey thought looked like a medical report. "Your honor, I have here a report that was done by the emergency department where Ms. Markum was taken following her injuries. I'd like to submit it at this time."

"Very well."

"You'll see that it indicates blood work was done. There was no reported alcohol in Ms. Markum's system. None." He turned to face Adams once again. "Mr. Adams, can you tell me what Ms. Markum was wearing that night? Was it particularly revealing or sexual in any way? You did say that this was to be a sexual encounter, is that correct?"

"I don't know what the hell she was wearing. That doesn't matter." He waved his hand dismissively.

Again, Gabriel drew a document from his briefcase. "The follow-up report indicates that Ms. Markum was wearing a plain, white blouse and black pants, no jewelry other than very small stud earrings and a watch. Hardly a get-up for a night on the town, wouldn't you say?"

"Well, I don't . . ."

"Mr. Adams, when the police searched your car after the incident, they found Ms. Markum's camera bag inside. Why did you have that with you?"

Audrey thought she noticed Adams's attorney trying to signal him somehow, but the man was focused on Gabriel's attack. "Hell, I figured I'd sell it, especially since she didn't put out after all I went through."

"Went through?"

"Yeah, the arrangements I made." Audrey caught her breath and held it, a bubble of hope forming in her chest.

"You made arrangements, Mr. Adams?"

"Sure, I wanted the night to go just right, didn't I?"

Gabriel folded his hands on the podium, first looking at the jury and then at the judge. "Nothing further, your honor."

The judge turned toward the defense table. "Defense?"

Adams's attorney stood in place, and Audrey thought that the woman looked less sure of herself than she had when she first walked in. "The Defense rests, your honor."

He banged his gavel. "Very well. Guards, please escort Mr. Adams out. We will take a twenty-minute recess and then resume with closing arguments.

It didn't look as though anyone was leaving the room as audience members stood and stretched, chatting in quiet groups. Audrey kept her back to the young reporter and went to sit at the table beside Gabriel. She leaned in close so that they wouldn't be overheard. "What do you think?"

"I think that attorney was an idiot for putting her client on the stand. That's what I think. But maybe she had no other choice." He shrugged. "We shall see."

"Do you think people believed all of that, that I'd go to a club and ask someone about violent sex?"

Gabriel laughed and took both of Audrey's hands in his. "Audrey, trust me. There is not a person on this planet who would look at you and think that any of what he said was possible. He's hung himself out to dry, pure and simple. I'm not a betting man, but if this goes to the jury today, I predict we'll have a verdict before dinner time."

Audrey thanked him and felt her shoulders falling back into place as she returned to her seat. It wasn't long before the judge and jury returned. It was Gabriel's turn to speak first.

"Ladies and gentlemen of the jury. I told you at the beginning of this trial that it was going to be simple and brief. You have seen that for yourself today. In her sensible white shirt and black pants, with her camera bag in tow, Ms. Markum was working that Friday night. She was not drunk and heading to an apartment for violent sex with a man old enough to be her father. In the days leading up to this vicious attack, you have heard how Mr. Adams stalked Ms. Markum, how he rented an apartment across the street from hers and sent a pointed message to her via the market. Then, that Friday night, he waited outside her apartment, assaulted her, then marched her across the street at gunpoint. He marched her, in fact, to an apartment where a chair and rope were already prepared so that she could be tortured and ultimately killed. In his own words, Mr. Adams stated that he had made his arrangements, ladies and gentlemen, made his arrangements. That is the very definition of premeditation. He stalked her, he attacked her, he beat her until her nose was broken and her face was bloodied, then he stuffed cleaning cloths in her mouth and tied a bandanna around her face, knowing that she could not breathe. Finally, when he was convinced that she was dead, he cut her loose, threw her to the floor, and returned the chair to its place in the bedroom. Then he went and got a little breakfast."

Gabriel paused, and Audrey looked at the jury. Many pairs of eyes seemed to be shifting back and forth between Gabriel and Adams. "He then took a drive to a neighborhood where he used to live, and he pulled up in front of the house where Ms. Markum's parents live. When the police closed in, he fired at Officer Chao's partner. Luckily for all of us, Mr. Adams was stopped before he could hurt anyone else. Attempted murder and aggravated assault are two very serious charges, ladies and gentlemen. There is no question at all that Mr. Adams is guilty of both. Thank you."

He sat down, and Adams's attorney stepped to the podium. "Ladies and gentlemen, the prosecutor would like you to think that this is a simple open and shut case. Let me assure you, it is not. What the police and prosecution have is a list of coincidences, that is all. There is no evidence that my client was in the coffee shop, as Ms. Markum stated, and, as far as I know, it's not a crime to tell someone hello. That's it. That's what the prosecution would like you to think amounts to stalking. And may I remind you, there were no fingerprints in the apartment, no witnesses to the supposed attack on Ms. Markum, nor does anyone report seeing my client pointing a gun at her. The evidence just does not bear up to close scrutiny. It is a house of cards, ladies and gentlemen, that is all, and I am confident that you will see through it. There's simply no case to be made here. Thank you."

The woman returned to her seat, but as Audrey watched, it almost looked like she was backing away from Adams slightly as if maybe she was glad that her work with him was done. Then Audrey's phone vibrated in her back pocket, and her attention was drawn away.

Rod started the engine as he turned to talk with Smitty. "Scout'll be out front at the courthouse. Trial's done."

"My God, she's going to be so glad it's over, isn't she? I hope they give the bastard life."

"Well, they have to find him guilty first, but yeah, I'm with you. I definitely don't want him getting back out and pulling that shit all over again." They were in front of the courthouse within a few minutes, and Rod pulled up to the curb. As Audrey opened the back door and climbed in, Smitty twisted around to apologize.

"Sorry, police business or I'd let you ride shotgun."

"No problem." She clipped her seatbelt into place, and they were moving. "Where are we going?"

"Julius Dudnyk's house," Smitty answered. "Back up is right behind us."

Rod could hear her take in a quick breath. "Do you think Rosey's there?"

He hated how hopeful her voice sounded and regretted having dragged her into it. "Scout, we just don't know what we'll find. But we thought that if Rosey is there, you'd be able to recognize her. Am I right?"

"Of course."

"All right, that's good, but you have to stay in the truck until we're sure it's safe, understand?" Rod reached his hand back and clasped hers for a quick moment.

"I can do that."

"All right." Rod put both hands back on the wheel and picked up speed.

"Getting into position now." The radio crackled, and Rod looked around him as they entered the subdivision. He spotted the two cars that were flanking the house and assumed that the third was in position around back. He pulled up next to the driveway and stopped. He and Smitty checked their guns and then returned them to their holsters before stepping away from the vehicle. They walked together up to the front door, both scanning the house ahead of them and the yard all around.

"Nothing in the windows that I can see. You?"

"Nah, nothing."

"Okay, here goes nothing. Be ready." Rod rang the doorbell, and they listened as it echoed inside the house. There was no response. The two men waited, and then Rod rang the bell again. This time he thought that he heard a crying sound. He looked at Smitty and whispered. "Do you hear that?"

Smitty nodded and stepped away from the doorway as he spoke into his radio. "Captain, we've got no response, and we think we hear a baby crying. We clear to go in?"

Rod watched as Smitty listened to the response. Then he looked up at Rod. "He says we've got the go to enter. How do you want to do this?" He tested the handle but found it locked.

"You up to helping me kick in a door? Seems like the easiest way in."

"I gotcha." They pulled out their guns. "Come on, on the count of three." He counted it down, and together they each landed a heavy boot in the middle of the door. The wood around the latch splintered, and they were in. They paused and the air filled with the sound of a baby crying. Smitty gestured to Rod to go right, and he moved left. As they entered each room, they called out 'clear' as one room after another proved to be empty. Once that floor had been checked, they headed up the stairs.

The screaming was much louder here. Rod peeked into what looked like a master bedroom, but it too was empty. They moved to the next door where the crying was coming from and opened it carefully. There in the crib lay an infant crying, the bodies of a man and woman lay crumpled on the floor.

"Jesus," Smitty said, then put two fingers along the woman's jawline while Rod did the same with the man.

"I got nothing. You got anything?" Rod said.

"Yeah, maybe. Call for an ambulance while I go talk to the captain. I'll bring in Audrey."

"You got it." The man's body seemed to have pulled the woman out of the rocking chair, so Rod pushed him aside and stretched the woman out on the floor. He bent closer and thought that perhaps he was seeing her chest move. He could detect a heartbeat, but it was faint. He figured it would be a crapshoot whether or not the ambulance would get there in time.

The man was gone, and there was nothing he could do for the woman now, so he turned and bent over the crib, picking the screaming baby up and stepping away from the bodies on the floor. "Well, I seem to remember Rosey screaming like this. Is that who you are, little one?" He stepped out of the room just as Audrey was coming up the stairs.

"Is it her?" She breathed out.

"You tell me, Scout. Here." He handed the baby to Audrey and watched as her eyes filled with tears.

"Rosey baby, it's me. Oh, honey." Rod watched as she held the baby close to her chest while tears streamed down her face.

"I take it that's a yes?" Rod laughed, and Audrey joined him.

"Yes, yes." She laughed. "She needs a change, and I'd bet money she's hungry, but yes, this is Rosey."

Just then, Smitty called up to them from downstairs. "Ambulance is on its way. Is it her? Is it Rose?"

Rod called down. "Scout says it is!"

"Oh, thank the Lord!" He shouted over his shoulder to the captain. "It's her! We've got her!"

He followed Smitty up the stairs, and the three of them surrounded Audrey as she cuddled the baby to her. Then they heard the siren, and Smitty ran down to direct them. Rod, Audrey, and the baby followed after him. Later, they were all downstairs on the sidewalk when the EMTs came down with the woman on the stretcher. "She gonna' make it?" Rod asked as they moved past him to the back of the ambulance.

"We've got her for now, but we're not sure for how long. We'll send another wagon for the body." With that, the doors were shut, and they took off, the siren piercing through the quiet of the neighborhood.

Rod looked at the captain. "What's the protocol here, Captain? Can we just take her home?"

He shook his head. "Sorry, we have to get her checked out by a doctor first. I trust Audrey here, but we'll have to get more definitive proof before we approach the parents."

Smitty spoke up then. "I've got the name of the baby's pediatrician. Why don't we see if they'll check her out? I bet they'll have records to help identify her, too."

"Good idea," the captain agreed. "You three go and do that while I finish up here. I know you're invested in this case, and if it turns out the way we hope it will, I want you all to be able to enjoy it."

"Great," Rod agreed. Smitty had stepped away and was already on the phone. One set of officers stayed while the other two cars were sent on their way.

"We need some supplies, Rod. And some kind of carrier if we can find one." Audrey added.

"Right." He started inside, but the second ambulance pulled up then, so they went to check with them first. They had diapers and milk, so Audrey laid her on the back seat of Rod's truck to change her.

Smitty had the phone in his hand, covering the mouthpiece as he spoke with Rod. "The doctor is thrilled that we think we've found her. He wants to come here right away."

Rod nodded. "Ask him if he's got a car seat we can borrow."

Smitty stepped away again but returned quickly. "We're all set. He's coming here with a seat, and then he'll follow us back to his office. He says he's got birth records including footprints that he thinks will confirm her identity."

Rod looked at where Audrey was sitting in the back seat. She was offering Rosey the small bottle of milk that the EMTs had shared with them. Rod and Smitty moved to stand by the open door. "I don't think the identity is going to be much of an issue here, do you?"

"Nope." Smitty offered before going back inside to talk with the other officers.

Fifteen minutes later, the doctor arrived. They fastened the car carrier into Rod's back seat and settled the baby into it, then trailed the doctor back to his office and relinquished the baby to his nurse. "How long will it be?" Audrey asked the doctor before he turned back to the examining room.

"Not long." He left then, and the three of them stepped back outside to discuss what to do next.

"Should we have Sandy and her husband come here?" Rod asked both Smitty and Audrey.

"Well, if the doctor can't ID her, then they'll have to, I think," Smitty answered.

"If he can confirm that it's Rosey, it'd be a lot easier for us to take her to them than it would be for them to bundle Martha up and bring everyone here." Audrey gestured toward Rod's truck. "Especially since we already have a car seat that we can use."

They discussed it for a few minutes longer before a nurse appeared at the door and motioned them back inside. The doctor came out carrying the baby and handed her back to Audrey. "I can officially attest that one, this baby is healthy, and two, that she is Rose Marie Wilder-Jones. The footprint is a match."

"Oh, thank God. I knew it!" Audrey held the baby up in the air and watched as a perfect smile began to form on her small face. "Let's get you home, little one. Right now!"

"Amen to that, brother." Smitty slapped Rod on the back, and the three of them headed back out the door.

As they pulled up to Sandy and Oscar's house, Audrey looked at Rod. "Did either of you call and tell them that we were coming?"

The two men looked at each other and shook their heads. "Nope," Rod answered.

"We figured we'd just knock on the door," Smitty added.

Audrey headed through the garage toward the side door. We don't even have to do that." She opened the door and called out. "Sandy!"

48

"Audrey, we're in the den. What's up?" Sandy called from the other room, and Audrey could hear someone getting up and moving toward them.

Audrey spotted her mother in the kitchen as she turned at the sound of the door. A look of shock was on her face, but Audrey held her finger up to her lips. "Shh." Brigitte stepped back next to the counter where she could see but be out of the way, her hand covering her mouth to keep from calling out.

Sandy appeared in the kitchen doorway with Martha in her arms. "Oh, my God!" She screamed, scaring a cry out of both babies. "Oscar! Mama!"

Audrey could hear Oscar pounding down the stairs, and she could see Cecelia doing her best to move toward them, shuffling as quickly as she could despite the pain.

"Trade you," Audrey said as she handed Rose to Sandy and took Martha from her in turn.

"I can't believe it. She's here." Sandy looked at Rod and Smitty with tears covering her face. "I can't believe you two did it. You found my baby for me."

Martha began to squirm, and Audrey was struggling to keep a grip on her when she noticed that what the baby was trying to do was get to her sister. "Oh, honey." Audrey moved closer so that Martha could reach out a hand and grab hold of Rosey's arm. At once, both babies stopped crying. Oscar and Sandy smiled through their tears.

"You missed your sister so much, didn't you, Martha?" Oscar reached in to kiss both little girls on the cheek.

Sandy wasn't about to let Rosey out of her arms yet, but the group managed to shift to the living room where Oscar and Sandy could sit together, a child in each of their laps, while Cecelia and Brigitte huddled nearby.

"Unbelievable." Oscar looked at both men. "I still can't believe it. I kept telling myself that she was gone, that I had to get used to the idea and help everyone else move on, too. But I was struggling. And now . . ." He shook his head but couldn't find any more words.

Sandy was brushing at her tears. "She looks good, healthy. Where did you find her?"

Smitty tugged at the edge of Rose's small sock. "She was just outside the city in a house with a fully stocked nursery. It looked to us as though she'd been taken care of."

"The man who took her from the daycare center seemed to have brought her to his own home. There's a lot that we still don't know, of course, but we'll keep you all informed." Rod added.

Audrey's phone buzzed in her pocket, and she pulled it out to see the text. She looked up at Rod before stepping into the other room. When he joined her, she said, "The jury's coming back in. There's a verdict."

"Do you want to be there?"

Audrey thought about it for half a second, then put her shoulders back and stood as straight as she could. "Yes, I think I do. Would you mind driving me?"

"Not at all." They returned to the living room. "Sandy, Oscar, everyone, you have no idea how happy it makes us to bring Rosey home. I know we'll see you again soon, but we're going to take off now," Rod announced.

"The jury's just come in, and I want to be there," Audrey added.

"Wow, so soon? Of course, go, go, go." Sandy stood up; Rosey still tucked into her arms. "But you better get back over here this weekend so we can celebrate!" There were tears and hugs all around the room before they were allowed to go.

When they got outside, Rod turned to his partner. "Smitty, do you mind riding with us to the courthouse?"

"Hell no. I want to hear this too, Audrey." He stepped back and grinned. "You've got shotgun, girl." Audrey laughed and climbed into the seat beside Rod. "Let's hit it," Smitty called from the back, and they were on their way.

Rod stuck the light on the roof, and they made quick work of the drive to the courthouse. They left the vehicle in a restricted area and hurried up the stairs. They were just settling into seats in the back row when Adams and then the judge re-entered the chamber.

"All rise." Everyone stood, and Audrey took Rod's hand. Once everyone was seated again, the judge spoke. Audrey couldn't tell if he still looked as giddy as he had in the beginning or not. At any rate, it didn't matter. "Has the jury reached a verdict?" He asked.

The jury foreman, a blonde-haired man about the age of Audrey's father, stood and handed the bailiff a slip of paper, which he took to the judge. The judge read it and then returned it to the foreman. The judge spoke. "On the first count, aggravated assault against two officers of the law?"

"We find the defendant guilty, your honor."

Audrey couldn't see Adams's face from where she was sitting, but she could see that he'd dropped his head.

"And on the second count, attempted murder in the first degree?"

"Guilty, your honor, we find him guilty."

Even as the judge was dismissing the jury and Adams was being led out, the room had come to its feet. Audrey turned to Rod and was swept up into his arms. "You did it, Scout. You did it."

He put her down, and Smitty wrapped her in a hug as well. "Wow, this day just gets better and better, doesn't it?"

As they were making their way toward the door, a woman touched Audrey on the arm. "Could I have a quick word?" She asked quietly.

Audrey stepped away from Rod and into the open row where they could face each other. In an instant, Audrey recognized her.

"I wanted to thank you, Ms. Markum, for your strength and your bravery. You stood up to my husband in a way I never could."

"Mrs. Adams, I'm so glad to see you. You look well."

"I'm trying to put myself back together. I guess you could say." She waved her arm to indicate the room around them. "It's not Mrs. Adams anymore. It's Lois Green, and this, all of this helps. I won't have to disappear, thanks to you." A woman with the same brown hair and eyes stepped up then, and together they moved to go. Audrey put her hand on the woman's arm, just as she had done earlier.

"Ms. Green, Lois, Toby was a good friend to me. I still miss him."

"So, do I dear, so do I." She was gone then, her sister's hand gripped in her own.

"Who was that?" Rod asked, stepping next to Audrey.

Audrey turned and wrapped her arms around him once more. "That was the little boy's mother. She's alive, and she doesn't have to be afraid of Adams now."

"Thanks to you. Like Smitty said, better and better."

As Audrey was getting dressed to go to dinner at Rod's house, she was shocked to think how recently Simple Simon's funeral had been. In less than a month, everyone's world had been turned on its head and then righted once again. It was hard to fathom. She flipped through her closet, considering one outfit after another before deciding on a flowered sundress. The day was warm, and she thought that the flowers might inspire a good mood. For some reason, she'd been struggling with that recently.

She didn't have a photograph to take Rod this time, but she did have her overnight bag as well as her camera bag and laptop. She was looking forward to spending time with him, but with everything that had been going on, she'd gotten a little behind in her work. She needed to put together at least two photographic packages that weekend. Then, there were weddings lined up for the next four weekends in a row as everyone tried to take advantage of the late summer weather. She needed to be ready. As she stepped out of her apartment door with bags draped over both of her arms, she froze, terror sweeping through her as her heart raced and she fought to breathe. She fell back against her apartment door and tried to practice what the counselor had begun to teach her, but the battle was raging at a chemical level inside her body. Her brain was making little progress trying to bring it under control. After what felt like a very long time, she finally began to breathe more normally and noticed that her phone was buzzing.

She set down two of the bags and pulled the phone out as she continued to count through her breathing. Her ride was there. Slowly and deliberately, Audrey gathered her bags back up and made her way over the threshold to the outside. The sun was shining, and a kind-looking woman was standing by a car with its door open. Damn it all, when would this stop, she wondered? As she set her bags inside and climbed in after them, she managed to make a little bit of small talk with the driver, but all the time, she was yelling at herself inside. Why couldn't she make it stop? Adams was gone. His sentencing would be in three weeks, and the expectation was that he'd be given life. But her rational brain seemed to have little control over her irrational self. It was maddening. The counselor had warned her that the apartment building might be just too strong of a trigger to overcome. Audrey hated to think that, but perhaps the woman was right. She pulled her phone out and began to look for apartment listings as they made their way out to Brookline.

When she got there, Rod was down the stairs quickly and took over most of the bags she'd brought before leaning in to kiss her. "I'm glad you're here! Far's been checking the window every five minutes and yelling out his reports to us." He tilted his head to the side as he looked at her. "You all right?"

Audrey forced herself to put it all out of her mind and enjoy the evening. She could look for listings in the morning. "I'm good, just a little tired. I'm looking forward to seeing Far again. Is he still after you to get a new dog?"

"No, actually, he hasn't mentioned it. I wonder what that means?"

They went inside, and Rod took a moment to carry Audrey's bags back to the bedroom. While he was gone, his sister Emma stepped toward her with open arms. "Audrey, Rod told us everything. Such wonderful news!" Audrey was swept into a hug and then passed to Gina once she entered the room as well. Far had no interest in the hugging but plopped down on the ottoman in front of Audrey as soon as the room quieted down.

"Beer anyone?" Rod asked before pointing at Far. "Not you, goofy."

"I'll take one," Audrey answered, as did Emma.

"Just water for me, please," Gina answered, and Audrey caught a look pass between the two women. Then she noticed that Far was practically jumping out of his skin as he fidgeted in his seat. When Rod returned and handed the drinks around, apparently, it was a signal of some sort because the little boy jumped to his feet and went to stand in front of his mothers.

"Okay, bud. You can spill it." Gina smiled and poked him in the back.

"I'm going to be a big brother!"

Rod looked at his sister first, but she shook her head. "Not me this time, Gina's turn."

Rod quickly bent down and engulfed his sister-in-law in a gentle hug. "This is awesome news, Gina. How are you feeling? When are you due?"

Before she could get a word out, Far announced, "The baby's going to come on my birthday!"

"Aw, buddy, that is fantastic!" Rod swept the little boy up and swung him around in a circle.

They settled back into their seats then, and the conversation spun off into different areas, but Audrey didn't find herself adding much to the discussion. Emma and Gina's family was growing, and clearly, all of them were thrilled, but it made something ping deep inside Audrey as she thought about her life and where she was going.

Her wedding photography business was doing well. The requests were starting to fall into a reasonably steady stream. Although she knew she couldn't give up the police work entirely, especially if she was going to be looking and paying for a new apartment, perhaps she could start to think about cutting back her hours. On the other hand, though, maybe she'd look for a place that was a little nicer with a deck or a patio or something so that she could have some outdoor space to herself.

Soon the group decamped to the kitchen and the back yard where Rod started the grill, and Emma and Far began kicking around a soccer ball. Once everything had been brought out to the table, Audrey joined in. Far was quick and seemed to move well for such a little guy. "Emma, Gina, this guy is a soccer player!" Audrey said as they all returned to the porch and prepared to eat.

"I'm going to be on a team when school starts this fall!"

"You're going to school?" Audrey asked. "Really?"

"Of course! I'm going to be in kindergarten. I hope our team is called the Sharks. I really like sharks." He was off on a lengthy recitation of shark facts that Audrey enjoyed but thought might require a little Googling later for confirmation. He was a happy child, though, and that made Audrey feel good. She pictured her friends with their two little girls and thought that they would be close in age to Far's new sibling. Wouldn't it be nice if maybe they all got to know each other?

The evening didn't go too late, and with everyone helping to clean up, Emma, Gina, and Far were heading out the door before nine. After one last round of hugs and congratulations, the house grew quiet, and Audrey and Rod were on their own once again. They split a beer between them and moved to the back porch, sitting side by side with their feet propped up on the rail. The traffic noise still echoed from down the hill while a half-moon was beginning to appear through the wispy clouds.

"Okay, Scout. Now you spill it. What's going on?"

"Aw Rod, is it that obvious? I'm sorry."

"It's just obvious to me." He picked up her hand. "They didn't notice. Believe me. They are in a world of their own right now."

"Are you happy about their news?"

"I am. I think Far will make a great big brother, don't you?"

Audrey smiled. "I do. I love how enthusiastic he is. I never had any brothers or sisters, so I'm a bit envious of him. It's kind of like watching Martha and Rose cuddling together. You know that their whole lives, they're going to have this other person connected to them. Just like you and Emma."

"You're right. It is nice. But you haven't answered my question. What's bothering you?"

Audrey set the glass on the table and shifted in her seat to face Rod. "On my way here, I had another panic attack, a bad one. It just makes me so mad. The trial is over, he's gone for good, but I still can't get over the fear. On my way over, I started looking at some listings for apartments. I think I might try to find something with a deck or a patio, maybe." She gestured at the yard in front of them. "I miss having some outdoor space and, if that damned threshold is the only trigger I have left, which, it seems like it is, then, two birds with one stone, I guess. What do you think?"

"Audrey, I like the plan, in part because I agree with you. Every time I go to pick you up there, I get a hit to my gut remembering what you looked like after the attack. So, I like the idea of a clean start, but not the idea of a new apartment."

"Why not?"

"When you got here today, you asked me if I'd decided to get a dog. I haven't. I don't want a new dog. I want you, here, every day with me. Would you consider moving in with me? I've been planning to tackle the back bedroom upstairs, and I thought I'd make it into an office. We could share it."

Audrey looked at Rod and leaned in to kiss him but wasn't quite sure what to say. Was it giving in to weakness somehow, not standing on her own two feet, facing her fears on her own?"

Rod leaned back. "I said that wrong. What I should have said first was, I love you, Audrey. I am wowed by you, by your strength, your toughness, your courage. And I would be thrilled if you'd move in with me, if you'd start to think about maybe sharing your life with me."

Audrey stood and pulled him to his feet, bringing her arms around him as they met together in the darkened space. She realized that she didn't feel weak or beaten by everything that had happened. Instead, she felt like herself and, if Rod loved her for that, then she'd love him right back. "I love you, too, Rod, and I would love to move in with you." In the back of her mind, Audrey thought, once she was moved in, perhaps she'd schedule a visit to the allergist. Maybe she would be okay with a dog.

A bright light was forcing Hannah to squint, and she realized with a shock that she was still alive. Then the grief swept over her, and she wrenched her head away from the brightness. A hand rested on her shoulder, and she opened her eyes to see a doctor with a small flashlight in her hand. She snapped it off.

Mrs. Dudnyk, Hannah, I'm Doctor McQuade. Do you know where you are?"

Hannah studied the doctor's face before tears flooded her eyes and the image blurred. She managed just a small nod.

"Mrs. Dudnyk, it's Tuesday morning now. You've been out for some time. Are you able to sit up a bit?"

Hannah summoned enough strength to lift her back and inch herself upwards. A nurse wedged a pillow behind her before stepping back. The doctor performed a series of tests then, checking her eyes and ears before using the stethoscope to listen to her heart and lungs. When she finished, she looped the stethoscope around her neck and straightened up. "Mrs. Dudnyk, you're doing very well. We're pleased. There are some detectives outside who'd like to speak with you if you're ready."

Hannah couldn't imagine ever being ready for that conversation. Would they arrest her? Would she be charged with helping Julius kidnap the child? Would she be alone and in jail? She felt herself sinking back down in the bed. What did it matter anyway?

The doctor had ushered the nurse out and was about to leave as well when she turned back. "I forgot to mention, Mrs. Dudnyk. The fetus seems to be doing quite well, with no ill effects as far as we can see. Of course, we'll want to monitor you well into the next trimester, but we're not too concerned."

She turned to go just as two men, one white and one black, started through her door.

"A baby?"

ACKNOWLEDGMENTS

A number of very special, longtime friends have kept me going through this writing and publishing process. They include many of my early readers as well as my walking companions, Dorothy Ebersole, Jan Weston, and Tina Ezekiel. In addition to them, the Wednesday morning crew of Jane Raymond, Lori Johnson, Alice King and Liz Rother have offered their unfailing support and encouragement. There is something so special about friends you've known for decades.

Once again, I'd like to especially thank the wonderful M. Karen Brawn for her excellent editing advice and insight. Her patience and thoughtful commentary made all the difference!

For their expertise, I'd again like to thank my friends Suzanne Biermann M.A, CCC-SLP Speech-Language Pathologist and Carol Fast MSPA, CCC-SLP, also a Speech-Language Pathologist. Their oversight and knowledge were invaluable. I'd also like to thank Carl Ent, former Chief of Police for Ann Arbor, Michigan for his expertise in the workings of police investigations and procedures.

As always, I'd like to thank my husband and the rest of my family for their unwavering love and support.

ABOUT THE AUTHOR

LINDA COTTON JEFFRIES grew up in Carlisle, Pennsylvania. She attended the University of North Carolina at Chapel Hill and taught special education for over thirty years. Her novels, *We Thought We Knew You* and *Who We Might Be*, were published recently by Fifth Avenue Press in Ann Arbor, Michigan. *Seeing in the Quiet*, the first in the Audrey Markum series, was published by Sunbury Press. Strong women, suspense, and romance are the elements she most enjoys writing about!

www.LindaCottonJeffries.com

www.ingramcontent.com/pod-product-compliance
Lightning Source LLC
Chambersburg PA
CBHW011407010726
47494CB00017B/2554